feasts from the PLACE below

Seasonal Celebrations From London's Top Vegetarian Restaurant

Bill Sewell

Thorsons

An Imprint of HarperCollins*Publishers*

Also by Bill Sewell:

Food From The Place Below

Thorsons
An Imprint of HarperCollins*Publishers*
77–85 Fulham Palace Road
Hammersmith, London W6 8JB

The Thorsons website address is:
www.thorsons.com

Published by Thorsons 1999

1 3 5 7 9 10 8 6 4 2

© Bill Sewell 1999

Bill Sewell asserts the moral right
to be identified as the author of this work

A catalogue record for this book is
available from the British Library

ISBN 0 7225 3729 8

Printed and bound in Great Britain by
Woolnough Bookbinding Ltd, Irthlingborough

Contents

Acknowledgements iv

Introduction vi

Basic Recipes x

January 1

February 22

March 44

April 66

May 84

June 105

July 124

August 153

September 166

October 189

November 205

December 226

Index 255

Acknowledgements

As I write, The Place Below is nearly 10 years old and the Café @ All Saints in Hereford is nearly two. Over the last 10 years a large number of people have helped me learn about food, cooking and restaurants and all of them have contributed (in many cases unwittingly) to this book. There is only room here to single out a few people to whom I am particularly indebted.

Ian Burleigh, who runs The Place Below, has looked after both me and the restaurant through thick and thin. His sensible attitude to food and his generous approach to life inform many of the recipes in this book. At the other side of the country, Julie Ayer, the manager of the Café @ All Saints, and Anthony Gardner, the head chef, have so thoroughly taken on the day-to-day running of the Café that I have had the freedom to sit at home testing recipes.

Past and present members of staff in both restaurants have made them the places they are. They have not only kept churning out huge quantities of delicious food and friendly welcomes, but have also been the source of many of the ideas in this book. Where recipes have clearly come from particular people I have tried to credit the original creator – my apologies for any failures of attribution.

It may not have escaped the reader's notice that both restaurants are in churches. In London the church is my landlord and in Hereford the business is owned by the church. In both London and Hereford the priests and congregations have been hugely supportive and have over the years been guinea pigs for many of the recipes in this book. So a particular thank you is due to Victor Stock, the Rector of St Mary-le-Bow and Andrew Mottram, the priest in charge at All Saints.

Thank you, also, to Gilly Cubitt and the team at BBC *Vegetarian Good Food* magazine, who have been enthusiastic supporters and promoters of the Café @ All Saints since before we opened our doors.

Neither book would have been written without the encouragement and also the bullying of my agent, Tessa Strickland. And it certainly would not have been published without the wholehearted support of my editor at Thorsons, Wanda Whiteley.

A large part of writing a book composed mostly of restaurant recipes is testing them in a domestic kitchen and home circumstances. As ever, friends and family have been willing tasters and, in a few cases, testers. A useful tip is to tell your friends you are writing a cookery book, invite them to dinner and then say that they have to cook it in order to test whether the recipe instructions make sense. Thank you Loo, Tom and Jo!

The process of testing recipes at home was made very much more pleasurable by the arrival of my new DCS domestic cooker. This huge piece of stainless steel is not only excellent and simple to cook with and extremely robust, but also so beautiful that I stroke it every morning when I come downstairs to make tea. (There is photographic evidence of me kissing tomatoes when I was four, so I've not really moved on much.)

Lastly I want to say a huge thank you to Sarah: for keeping enthused and excited about this project; making sure my words make sense; being a well-balanced critic and managing to combine all this with moving to the country **and** producing the most delicious and lovely baby I've ever met.

This book is dedicated to my parents, Robert and Jean, and to my son Jonathan whom they would have loved to meet.

Introduction

This is a cookbook about the pleasures of eating different things at different times. It is also a book which shows the rich and luxurious possibilities of celebratory vegetarian cooking.

Some, but by no means all, of the recipes are a little more ambitious than those in the first Place Below cookbook, especially those designed for big special occasions like Christmas dinner or Easter lunch. These are meals to cook when you have plenty of time and you really feel like a session in the kitchen. They may also require some thinking ahead on the shopping front – if, for instance, you haven't got a ready supply of truffle oil, samphire or nori. If there are more easily available alternatives, I have mentioned them in the recipes.

There are also many really simple and quick seasonal delights – pasta, and soup recipes that will fit snugly into an after-work routine; supper and salad recipes which will use up neither your life's savings nor your reserves of patience.

Seasonal eating

Most of us now live in ways which, to some extent, isolate us from changing seasons. We have centrally heated houses, air-conditioned offices and travel around by car. We shop in supermarkets where most vegetables are available for most of the year. We only register the weather when it interferes with Wimbledon or starts blowing trees on top of our houses. Traditional celebrations such as Christmas and Easter, Valentine's day and May Day seem more like opportunities for vigorous marketing than for seasonal feasting.

This book is a reminder of delicious differences. I don't want to turn the clock back – I like my central heating and my fridge as much as the next person does. But I do love the changes that a year brings – especially in Britain. Everything is not at its best all of the time. Early rhubarb starts in January and comes from Yorkshire. Our earliest asparagus can start as early as March in the west end of Cornwall and it will all be finished by the end of June. Samphire and strawberries; peas and potatoes; pumpkins and parsnips: all have their season of glory. They may be available at other times of year but they won't be so good and they will probably be much more expensive. You can buy Egyptian parsnips in August and Spanish strawberries in January. But why would you want to?

This is intended to be only the most gentle campaigning book – and I am campaigning to convert myself as much as other people. Moving towards a more genuinely seasonal approach is a slow process because we are all so deeply seduced into thinking that all food should be available to us whenever we want it.

So this is not a book for purists. You will find many dishes recommended which include ingredients not strictly in their natural season. But I hope you will also find that I have highlighted the most exciting and genuinely seasonal fruits and vegetables.

Seasonality is not only a question of what is available but also of what we *feel* like eating at different times of year. Chocolate is not a seasonal commodity, but I know both from my own tastebuds and from sales in my restaurants, that people eat more chocolate with more passion in the depths of winter than at the height of summer. So I have a short section on chocolate in February. Likewise, spiced vanilla ice cream can be made at any time of year, but you are more likely to want to eat it in summer, so you will find the recipe (along with some other delicious ice cream ideas) in the July chapter.

Where this book comes from

Although the book is called *Feasts from The Place Below*, this is shorthand. It should be called feasts, treats and seasonal favourites from The Place Below, The Café @ All Saints and Bill's kitchen. Probably the majority of the recipes come from seasonal dinners, wedding menus and other celebratory gatherings that we have hosted at The Place Below over the last 10 years. However, in the course of writing the book, I opened the Café @ All Saints in All Saints Church in Hereford, and some of the recipes come from there. Lastly, some of the recipes come from my everyday home cooking, still with a seasonal slant, but designed for eating when collapsed in front of the telly, rather than feasting at a candlelit table.

My favourite cookbooks all reveal both a love of food and something of the author's personality and life. This book particularly reflects the last two years of my cooking and eating life. During this time I opened the Café @ All Saints; Sarah and I moved from West London to a tiny village just outside Hereford; and we produced our first child, Jonathan. This does not mean that this is a book of ecclesiastical rural baby food (although that may be my next book!) but it does mean it is a book by a city boy beginning to discover the pleasures and challenges of country living.

Above all, this is a book of food to cook and experiment with. One of the more depressing things about the '90s is that despite the proliferation of food books and television programmes we all actually cook less and less. The exciting thing about the response to my first cookbook, Food from The Place Below, was the number of people who told me they cooked from it regularly, and I hope the same will be true of this book. The cake and bread recipes should be followed carefully to ensure good results. Many of the other recipes, on the other hand, should be starting points for your own food journeys. Your tastebuds and your own sense of what you find delicious should guide you as much as the recipes themselves.

May your mouths water and your tummies be full!

Note on ingredients and quantities

I won't repeat the fairly detailed notes I gave at the beginning of Food from The Place Below except to mention four essential ingredients.

Olive oil always means a decent but basic extra virgin olive oil.
Soy sauce means a dark soy sauce, naturally brewed, usually called 'shoyu' or (the wheat-free version) 'tamari'.
When tinned tomatoes are specified go for a good brand such as Napolina and ensure that the tin specifies that they are plum tomatoes.
A 'bunch' of herbs means a handful or so, about the size of a supermarket fresh herb packet.

Teaspoons and tablespoons are measured in level official teaspoons (5 ml) and tablespoons (15 ml) unless otherwise specified.

Each recipe specifies the number of people it serves, based on what I consider to be an average appetite. I had quite conflicting responses to the quantities in the first book, with some people feeling the portion sizes were on the large size and others feeling that their appetites were not fully catered for (sorry about that, Rob!). Different people eat different amounts, so my quantities are based on averagely hungry people eating the dish in the context in which it appears in the book – in other words a dish served as part of a seven-course feast will be smaller than if the same dish were served as a complete supper in its own right.

Basic Recipes

SWEET PASTRY

Pastry is not much hassle if you make enough for several tarts at a time. Divide it into the correct number of pieces, cover each in clingfilm and put the one for immediate use in the fridge and the others in the deep freeze. When you plan to use the frozen pastry, take it out of the deep freeze the day before you need it and put it in the fridge so that when it has defrosted it will be cool and ready to use. It is much more difficult to work with (in fact almost impossible) if you have defrosted it rapidly in the microwave.

Equally, if you are using it freshly made, it is essential to allow a couple of hours to let it chill thoroughly in the fridge before using. If you use it at room temperature it will fall apart; if you use it cold it's a joy to work with.

This pastry has a great tendency to slip down the tart shell when you are blind-baking it. To prevent this you should press into the sides of the tin very firmly and then get a duplicate tin and carefully press it down on top. So long as the sides of the tin slope out slightly, which they usually do, you can use the second tin to keep the pastry pressed firmly against the sides of the bottom one.

This pastry takes 10–15 minutes to bake blind (i.e. without any filling) at 200°C.

MAKES SUFFICIENT FOR THREE 23CM (9 INCH) OR TWO 30CM (12 INCH) TARTS

200 g (7 oz) unsalted butter
350 g (12 oz) plain white flour
75 g (3 oz) caster sugar
2 small eggs, lightly beaten

1. Whizz the butter and flour together in the food processor. Alternatively, rub the butter into the flour with the tips of your fingers, lifting the mixture as you do so, until it looks like breadcrumbs.

2. Add the sugar and whizz again or, if making by hand, rub the sugar in, too.

3. Add the eggs and whizz again, or mix them in thoroughly to gather the crumbs together into a dough. Divide the dough into three equal-sized pieces, cover in clingfilm and chill thoroughly before using.

WHOLEMEAL PASTRY

MAKES TWO 30CM (12 INCH) OR THREE 23CM (9 INCH) CASES

350 g plain wholemeal flour
175 g butter or hard vegan margarine
100 ml water
40 ml sunflower oil

1. Put the flour and butter or hard margarine into a blender. Whizz briefly —
   a couple of times should do it — until the mixture resembles breadcrumbs.
   You should not be able to see any separate bits of fat.

2. Leaving the machine going, pour in both the water and oil at once. The
   mixture should come together into a ball quite quickly. Stop the machine
   at this point. If you are used to making pastry, particularly white pastry,
   you may think that the mixture is too wet, but it isn't. The bran in the
   wholemeal flour will continue to absorb water as the dough rests.

3. Divide the pastry into two or three pieces (depending on which size of
   pastry case you are going to make) and wrap each ball of dough in clingfilm. Any you are going to use in the next day or two put in the fridge,
   while the rest can go in the freezer.

4. Even if the pastry is for immediate use, it must cool down and rest in the
   fridge for at least one hour, preferably longer. Do not try to roll it out
   immediately after making it, or you will have a nasty mess on your hands.

PESTO

Home-made pesto is radically different from the shop-bought variety. Once you have started making your own, you will not think of bottled pesto as the same thing at all. I have yet to find a shop-bought pesto which is worth bothering with. If you're in a hurry, have a look at the quick pasta suggestions on page 81.

MAKES 1.25 KG (2 LB 12 OZ) OR ABOUT 30 SERVINGS

4 large bunches of basil
2 large bunches flatleaf parsley
2 good cloves of garlic, peeled
225 g (8 oz) pine nuts
juice of 2 lemons
50 ml (2 fl oz) water
2 tsp salt
600 ml (1 pint) olive oil
350 g freshly grated Parmesan

1. Pick over the herbs, discarding all the thick stalks.

2. Put the garlic and pine nuts into a food processor and whizz to a fine powder.

3. Add the lemon juice, water, basil, parsley and salt and whizz until you have a smooth paste.

4. While still whizzing, pour in the olive oil, slowly.

5. Transfer the pesto to a large bowl and stir in the Parmesan. Check the seasoning. Keep in the fridge in an airtight container, ready to use as required.

JANUARY

New Year feast

Truffled scrambled eggs with roast parsnips

Field mushroom and cepe risotto

Salad of bitter leaves and oranges

Pear tarte tatin

New Year's resolution supper

Freshly squeezed orange juice or English apple juice

Daily sourdough

Sweet and spicy peasant soup

Compote of dried fruit with Greek yoghurt

Seasonal pleasure: marmalade

Uncle Tony's marmalade

New Year feast

To celebrate the New Year I want comfort and luxury – here it is!

Both the scrambled eggs and the risotto need to be cooked just before they are eaten, so this menu is good for a long spaced-out meal, where the cook can retire to the kitchen for a reasonable period of time between courses.

TRUFFLED SCRAMBLED EGGS WITH ROAST PARSNIPS

There are two elusive flavours which I have private and mostly futile crusades to re-experience as often as possible. One is the smell of the first really good glass of wine I drank (a Meursault, bought by my boss when I was learning to be an accountant). And the other is the taste of fresh truffles most deliciously remembered from a black truffle ravioli eaten on our honeymoon which we began in massive gastronomic luxury at Le Manoir aux Quat' Saisons.

Truffle oil is a good way of hinting at the peculiar earthy bliss of truffles (*see recipe on page 3*) but for this simple yet luxurious dish you need a good fresh truffle. Its surface should be a rich black and if you sniff it, it should have a strong whiff. If it is dried up and dusty-looking, don't bother. Black truffles are available (with difficulty) from December to February.

A revolution is currently happening in the world of truffles. It is whispered, even stated in newspaper articles, that they can now be cultivated. Don't get too excited. First, although this may mean that black truffles may become cheaper, they will not become cheap, since the cultivation process is slow and difficult. Second, I have a sneaking suspicion that the cultivated ones may not be as good. The best place I know to buy fresh truffles is our veg man at The

Place Below, Tony Booth, who has a fantastic shop just off Ludgate Hill in the City of London. This year in January, Tony was selling black truffles from France and China. The French ones were five times more expensive (at nearly £40 for 125 g) but they were far superior in flavour. Since even the most obsessive foodies won't be buying truffles every day, if you are going to splash out you must get the best you possibly can.

A truffle quest which has so far eluded me is to eat (and also cook with) Italian white truffles. I was determined that this year was to be my white truffle year. However, nature was not on my side. Dry weather at the wrong time in Italy meant that the price was approximately twice as astronomical as usual – so expensive that even Tony hasn't been buying them this year. That's the trouble with real wild food – it doesn't fit in with our need for instant gratification.

(If you can't get a fresh truffle, and, let's face it, most of us can't most of the time, then put the scrambled eggs on a roasted field mushroom, and surround by roast parsnips.)

SERVES 6 AS A STARTER

1 good black truffle
6 eggs
1 kg (2 lb 4 oz) parsnips
50 ml (2 fl oz) sunflower oil
Salt and freshly ground black pepper
75 g (3 oz) butter
80 ml (3 fl oz) milk

1. One or two days (not more) before you want to make the dish put the whole eggs in an airtight container with the truffle. (The shells of eggs are porous and this will really help intensify the flavour of the final dish. The same trick works with risotto rice and truffles.)

2. Pre-heat the oven to 220°C (425°F/Gas Mark 7). Peel the parsnips, quarter lengthways, and take out the core if it is woody.

3. Bring a large pan of water to the boil and put in the parsnips. Bring back to the boil, and simmer for about 10 minutes until the parsnips are just tender. Drain them well, and toss them in the sunflower oil with some salt and pepper. Spread out onto a large baking tray in a single layer and roast for about 30 minutes until just going golden but not crisp. Keep them warm while you do the rest of the dish.

4. Just before you make the scrambled eggs chop the truffle very finely and set aside. (Don't do this long in advance or the smell will evaporate.)

5. Make the scrambled eggs. Lightly mix the eggs in a bowl. In a pan, melt the butter and add the eggs and milk. Cook on a low heat, stirring constantly. Do not try to do anything else while making the scrambled eggs or you will overcook them, which will be frustrating if you have gone to a lot of trouble getting hold of a fresh truffle. When they are creamy but not quite set they are ready.

6. Divide the scrambled eggs onto warmed plates and sprinkle with the finely chopped truffle. Surround by roast parsnips. Mmmmmmm. (If you're really good eaters and your feast will be spread out over several hours you could serve the eggs on hot buttered crumpets.)

FIELD MUSHROOM AND CEPE RISOTTO

This dish is both simple and a real crowd-pleaser. We've served it at many parties at The Place Below when the hosts are worried about inviting carnivores to a vegetarian restaurant. This risotto has a depth of flavour reassuring to people who may still be expecting to be offered a low-fat nut cutlet and a lettuce leaf.

If you haven't yet experienced the heady smell of dried cepes (also called porcini mushrooms or, before we all became honorary citizens of the Mediterranean, penny buns) you are in for a treat. Like truffles (although not nearly as expensive) a little goes a long way. Unlike truffles, they are now available in most good delis and quite a few supermarkets. If you can find anywhere that sells them loose in decent quantities they are generally cheaper that way.

Serves 6

50 g (2 oz) dried cepes
500 ml (1 pint) hot water
500 ml (1 pint) red wine
1 tbsp soy sauce (more to taste)
50 ml (2 fl oz) olive oil
700 g (1½ lb) onions, halved and sliced (to give half rings)
3 cloves garlic, crushed
1 kg (2 lb) field mushrooms, thickly sliced
350 g (12 oz) risotto rice (e.g. arborio)
150 g (5 oz) freshly grated Parmesan

1. Soak the cepes in the hot water for about half an hour. Pick out the rehydrated cepes and set to one side. Pour the liquid through a fine sieve into a pan, trying to leave any grit at the bottom of the bowl. Add the red wine and soy sauce, bring to the boil and switch off.

2. In a large heavy-bottomed pan, heat the oil. Add the onions and cook over a medium heat. After about five minutes add the crushed garlic and a little salt. Continue cooking until the onions are very tender – perhaps another 10 minutes. Turn up the heat and add the field mushrooms. If you don't have a very large pan (you should get one) you may have to add the mushrooms a few at a time, stirring regularly.

3. Once the mushrooms have collapsed in size and have begun giving off their juices, add the rice and stir around for a couple of minutes. Turn the heat down to medium, add the rehydrated cepes and begin adding the hot wine mixture. Add the first ladleful and stir vigorously. Once that is largely absorbed add some more and continue this process until you have used up all the liquid. At this point the rice will probably not be quite cooked, so have a ready boiled kettle at hand to add a bit more liquid. Continue cooking until the rice is just cooked and there is a little liquid left in the pan – it should be slightly more solid than soup but not much. You need to keep close to the risotto while it is cooking or it will easily burn, and you must keep tasting the rice to see when it is ready. Stir in the Parmesan and serve at once.

SALAD OF BITTER LEAVES AND ORANGES

Chicory and orange is a classic combination. It's a good palate-cleanser after the rich risotto.

There are now lots of bitter and peppery leaves available, and this is an area where the organic vegetable box schemes are particularly strong. So use the best that's available to you whether that is the tight heads of blanched chicory or the fatter type of curly endive available in the winter, or a more peppery leaf such as rocket.

SERVES 6

2 heads chicory – preferably one red and one green, the leaves separated
Half a curly endive or some mizzuna or rocket
2 tbsp walnut oil
Salt and freshly ground pepper
4 large oranges, segmented

1. Toss the prepared leaves in walnut oil and season well.

2. Arrange the leaves on individual plates and divide the orange segments prettily between them. (If you serve the salad from a large dish at the table it is difficult to make sure that everyone gets their fair share of orange segments.)

PEAR TARTE TATIN

These caramelised upside-down tarts are a bit nerve-racking to make the first time, as you can't see what's going on at the crucial moment. But pluck up your courage and try one. Once you've got the hang of them they are simple, incredibly delicious and very versatile. Classically made with apples, I also use pears and quinces (the latter of which must be cooked first). Fresh fig and banana is an excellent autumn combination (*see page 211*).

There has also been a bit of a trend in fancy restaurants for savoury tartes tatins (made with chicory or baby onions) which sound wonderful but are generally a little disappointing.

To make a good tarte tatin you need a heavyweight pan that can also go in the oven. You can either spend a great deal of money on a special tarte tatin pan or (as brilliantly pointed out by the lady from the kitchenware shop in Richmond) buy a heavy deep pizza pan for less than half the price.

SERVES 8

75 g (3 oz) butter
140 g (5 oz) light muscovado sugar
900 g (1 lb) firm pears, peeled, cored and quartered
350g (12 oz) puff pastry (preferably all butter), thawed if frozen

1. Pre-heat the oven to 220°C (425°F/Gas mark 7). Gently warm the butter and sugar in a large ovenproof heavy-based frying pan (or pizza pan – see above) and when just melted, turn off the flame. Arrange the pears, flat side up, on top of the butter and sugar mixture.

2. Roll out the pastry to a circle just larger than the bottom of the pan and lay it over the pears. Pinch the pastry into the sides of the pan and make a few slits in the middle with a knife to allow steam to escape.

3. Place the pan over a medium flame and cook for about 10 minutes. This is the tricky bit – you want the sugar and butter mixture to caramelise with the pears but not to burn. Turn the heat too high and the mixture will burn, turn it too low and it will not caramelise. Your nose is probably the best guide – when you get a rich toffee smell this stage is complete. You can take careful peeks by lifting a corner of the pastry. When the fruit, sugar and butter have caramelised put the tart in the oven for about 15 minutes until the pastry is puffed up and golden brown. Carefully turn out, pastry-side down, on to a large flat serving dish and serve warm with clotted cream.

(If you find you haven't got a serving dish big enough to turn it out on to, a tray covered with foil will do fine.)

New Year's resolution supper

For the New Year you've been foolish enough to give up cheese, cream and butter but you still want to get pleasure from food and you've decided never again to buy horrible pappy factory-made bread. Here goes...

FRESHLY SQUEEZED ORANGE JUICE OR ENGLISH APPLE JUICE

Even the very best and freshest orange juice bought in a shop will not be as good as juice squeezed at home just before you drink it. (In February and March use Sicilian blood oranges if you can get them.) A piece from a Chaim Potok novel about a New Yorker who was obsessive about drinking his fresh orange juice as soon as he had squeezed it in order to get the maximum vitamin C benefit has always stuck in my head. Is it not another piece of providential nutritional planning that the best oranges are available in the months when we most need protecting against colds and flu?

However, since coming to live in Hereford my preferred morning-time drink has changed to apple juice. Not the blended and filtered commodity sold on the basis of cheapness in supermarkets, but locally pressed single variety juice. This may sound a bit airy-fairy and pretentious, but it really is a different drink. Quite a few fruit farms around Hereford produce their own single-variety juices with Red Pippin and Egremont Russet juices scoring highest on our family Richter scale. For both restaurants we buy Red Pippin juice from Hermitage Farm which is currently in conversion to fully organic production. Sadly, the more widely available James White single-variety juices from East Anglia are filtered and, in my view, not as interesting.

DAILY SOURDOUGH

Along with my quest for the taste of Meursault and the smell of truffles has been another long search – to make really good sourdough.

I tried at home on many different occasions, and always without success. David Goodyear, our baker at The Place Below, had a phase of making excellent rye sourdough, but I could never get it quite right. Finally, we had a bread class for our staff at All Saints with leading craft baker Paul Merry of Panary bakery consultancy (tel 017683 61102). His is the only telephone number I give in this book. He is a fantastic teacher and anyone who is interested in bread whether commercially or domestically, should make the time to go on one of his courses. He finally communicated to me the essentials of the sourdough process. Since then I have had a long phase of making sourdough at home every two or three days and all of us (including Jonathan when he was only six months old) have become addicted to it. For a time it has become more of a way of life than a recipe.

This is classic New Year's resolution bread. It is not that there is anything technically difficult about it, but initially it requires considerable reserves of patience, and is, quite frankly, difficult to combine with a full-time job. But given the choice between being able to eat delicious home-made sourdough and having a regular income, surely the answer is obvious?

The point of this kind of bread is that instead of introducing a yeast made as a by-product of the brewing industry, you leave the dough without any added yeast to pick up whatever yeasts are floating around in the atmosphere. These yeasts (unlike normal baker's yeast) thrive in a more acidic environment, which is exactly what is created as the dough is allowed to go sour. If you find the science and practice of this kind of thing interesting, then you should read *The Man Who Ate Everything* by Jeffrey Steingarten (Headline). He also beautifully illustrates the stresses and joys of home-production of sourdough: 'Thursday June 21... My wife feels that my baking schedule has prevented us going away on sunny summer weekends. She says it is like having a newborn puppy without the puppy. She has always wanted a puppy.'

Note two things before starting. First, don't forget to take a portion of your finished dough to use as a starter for your next batch. (I repeatedly failed to do this to begin with.) Secondly, remember that your first batch of bread will be the least successful. Thirdly, look after your leaven as though it were a favourite pet. It needs food and water, a good temperature and atmosphere, and not to be forgotten and left in a corner for too long.

Sourdough bread tends to be dense and chewy, so you should slice it very thinly. It makes wonderful toast, excellent sandwiches and keeps extremely well.

Paul Merry explains that there are three distinct phases to making sourdough:

- catching a wild yeast
- building up a leaven by refreshment
- making bread dough and cooking it

1. Catch a wild yeast

100 g (3½ oz) flour — roughly one third wholemeal and two thirds white
250 ml (9 fl oz) lukewarm water

Make a paste of the flour and water in a small mixing bowl or jar. If you live in an area where the tap water is heavily chlorinated use filtered or spring water; or use the tap water after it has sat in a jug overnight, by which time the chlorine gas will have dissipated.

Allow the wet paste to sit at room temperature. Do not put it in a cool place like a cellar or a larder. Loosely cover the bowl or put it inside a large plastic bag so that nothing drops into it. After only two or three days your wild yeast should be showing itself with clusters of fine bubbles of gas visible in the paste. It may not smell very pleasant and will look unpleasantly grey. It is now called the leaven.

2. Building up the leaven by refreshment

a) Nurturing the leaven in a sloppy state. This is where the nurture of your pet begins. The wild yeasts which you have captured need flour, water and warmth to multiply and become vigorous. The leaven must be fed every second or third day.

At the start the refreshment (the technical term for the feeding of your pet leaven) can be viewed as thirds: one-third leaven, one-third fresh flour, one-third water. Having the water content as high as a third will mean that it stays as a wet paste. The 200g of starter will now become a wet paste of 600g.

A couple of days later this 600g will be increased to 1.8kg. To avoid building up a vast ever-growing quantity, each refreshment must be preceded by throwing (or giving) away at least half or two-thirds of the leaven.

After several of these refreshments, perhaps three, four or five, you should see bubbling activity. Note that to reach this point may have taken as long as two weeks from your starting point. If you rush to make bread before the leaven has become vigorously bubbly, your loaves will only be a disappointment.

b) Converting the sloppy leaven to its properly textured permanent self. It is now time to turn the wet paste into a firmer, more dough-like leaven. You could even try it out at raising a loaf of bread. The smell of the leaven at this point will be vinegary or perhaps cheesy, but don't panic — that won't be the smell of the finished bread.

Previously when you were refreshing the sloppy leaven you used a refreshment of one third leaven, one third flour and one third water. To convert the sloppy leaven to a proper leaven you will need to reduce the amount of water to perhaps one sixth on the first occasion. But you have to use your hand and eyes to tell you when a dough-like texture has been achieved.

After this first occasion when you have turned the wet paste (sloppy leaven) into a dough-like ('proper') leaven the routine refreshment will be as follows:

300 g (10½ oz) proper leaven
300 g (10½ oz) flour (say two thirds strong white and two thirds wholemeal)
150–200 ml (5–7 fl oz) water

These are not robotic numbers – different flours and different atmospheres require slightly different quantities. You are looking to retain a dough-like consistency in your leaven.

These figures are the guidelines for the permanent management of your leaven. To keep it lively during the period when you do not wish to make bread it must still have regular refreshment every few days – every second or third to keep it in good shape. If you know that there will be a prolonged break from bread making it can live in the refrigerator. Every week or two, take it out, leave it for a day to achieve room temperature, refresh it, then it can go back to the fridge.

3. Making bread dough and cooking it

Your normal 300 g of proper leaven would convert to 800 g of refreshed leaven (see quantities in (b) above). Take 500 g of it to make bread, keeping back 300 g to continue as your pet leaven to be fed and watered every couple of days. Don't forget to keep back the 300 g of leaven or you will have to start the whole process all over again!

For one large loaf of Paul Merry's French Country Bread:

500 g (1 lb 2 oz) leaven
500 g (1 lb 2 oz) flour (one-third wholemeal, two-thirds strong white)
15 g salt
300–350 ml (10–12 fl oz) water

1. Mix the ingredients into a dough, making any adjustments of either flour or water that will result in a firm and pliable dough. Knead until you develop the gluten and the dough feels strong and stretchable like any good bread dough should.

2. Make the dough into a round shape and place in a proving basket. You can improvise a French proving basket by placing a well-floured cotton cloth into a mixing bowl. Leave it to prove for several hours, well covered, at normal room temperature. After 4 or 5 hours (longer if your kitchen is very cool) it should have proved well enough to be ready for baking. Heat the oven to 240°C (450°F). Turn the proved loaf gently out on to a lightly greased baking sheet and bake for 40–50 minutes. It should have a thick crust with a chewy textured crumb.

Enjoy it and tell everyone who will listen about how delicious it is and what a genius you are. It's a long, long recipe, but if you're converted it will stay with you for the rest of your life (at least that's what I'm hoping).

SWEET AND SPICY PEASANT SOUP

This kind of soup is a real pleasure to make on a cold day. Garlic, chilli and ginger sizzling in olive oil and then a wine-dark stock (as Homer would have said) bubbling away. A soup to clear out every orifice – a sort of spicy winter minestrone.

All sorts of unpromising bits of vegetable lurking in dark corners of your kitchen can happily go into it. Onions which are past their best, or slightly tired leeks, are fine. It is good with fennel as well as, or instead of, celery, and Swiss chard is a fine alternative to spring greens.

Large chunks of bread – preferably the first batch of sourdough from your New Year's bread-making resolution – are essential for wiping the plate.

Don't be put off by the long list of ingredients. It's a simple soup to make.

SERVES 6

100 g (4 oz) red lentils
100 g (4 oz) Puy lentils
200 g (8 oz) potatoes, finely diced
1 litre (2 pints) water

3 cloves garlic, peeled
1 hot red chilli with seeds (less or more to taste)
5 cm (2 inches) root ginger, peeled
75 ml (3 fl oz) olive oil + 2 tbsp

200 g (8 oz) red onion, finely diced
½ head celery, finely diced
200 g (8 oz) carrots, finely diced

500 ml (1 pint) red wine
2 tbsp soy sauce
2 tbsp dark muscovado sugar
300 g (10 oz) spring greens, finely shredded

1 x 400 ml (14 fl oz) can of coconut milk

1. Put the two kinds of lentils into a pan with the finely diced potatoes and the water. Bring to the boil and simmer for about 40 minutes until both kinds of lentils and the potatoes are tender (the orange lentils will have gone a bit mushy by this point). Don't try putting the potatoes in later with the wine, because the acidity of the wine will stop the potatoes from cooking properly.

2. Put the garlic, chilli and ginger with 75 ml (3 fl oz) olive oil into a blender and whizz to a rough purée. Set to one side.

3. In a large soup pan sweat the onions, celery and carrots in the remaining olive oil until half tender. Add the garlic/chilli/ginger puree and a good pinch of salt and continue cooking until the vegetables are tender. Adding the garlic etc. at this stage rather than cooking it before putting the veg in the pan gives the final soup extra punch.

4. Add the lentil mixture and the remainder of the ingredients including the spring greens but not the coconut milk. Bring to the boil and simmer for about 15 minutes until the spring greens are tender. Then add the coconut milk and re-heat but do not boil. Serve at once or whenever you've finished doing your New Year's resolution aerobics.

COMPOTE OF DRIED FRUIT
WITH GREEK YOGHURT

We have tried to sell winter fruit compote in both London and Hereford and have never succeeded. I think this is a pity because it is a dessert which seems to me both luxurious and virtuous.

You can use either normal dried fruit, or the ready-to-eat, moister kind. The tea might seem an odd thing to use, but it adds a depth of flavour without actually ending up tasting of tea at all (except to those of you with Jilly Goulden-style sensitive palates).

SERVES 6

500 g (1 lb 2 oz) mixed dried fruit
e.g. peaches, pears (my two favourites), apricots, prunes, figs
500 ml (18 fl oz) Earl Grey tea (made with one tea bag)
Piece of lemon peel

1. Put all the ingredients in a heavy-bottomed pan. Bring to the boil, cover and simmer for about 30 minutes. Leave to cool. Serve either at room temperature or chilled. Delicious either as it is or with Greek yoghurt or (if you've had enough of virtue) really thick cream.

Seasonal pleasure: marmalade

Not only are oranges from Israel at their juicy best this month, but all kinds of other citrus fruits wing their way towards us in the depths of winter. Before Christmas and a bit after there are satsumas, giving way to clementines, minneolas and blood oranges in January and February.

But closest to the hearts of gastronomically literate Britons are Seville oranges, available for only a few weeks in January, disgusting to eat raw but the essential ingredient for the only marmalade worth bothering with. Grapefruits and limes are wonderful fruits, but only useful for marmalade if war breaks out with Spain and we can't get Sevilles.

UNCLE TONY'S MARMALADE

Sarah and I saw a lot of 'Big Toe' when we were staying in Cornwall to write my first cookbook, and this marmalade recipe was just one of many delicious things he gave us.

We have made this marmalade for the last three years. Each time it has been delicious and each time slightly different. That is of course part of the point of making your own marmalade. It may sound pretentious, but there is a rich variety of tastes of marmalade in the same way that wine from the same grape variety will taste different from year to year. You can also choose how thick you like your peel to be in marmalade and whether you like it pale, fruity and aromatic or dark and sticky. There is a curious recipe in a well-known book on winter cookery which suggests that you should boil the marmalade for two hours – horrible, in my view, but an indication of how pleasurably personal marmalade can be.

If you are making anything with marmalade (*e.g. Chocolate and Marmalade Tart on page 42*), it will be significantly nicer if you use decent home-made marmalade.

Because Sevilles are mainly grown for British marmalade makers they are not sprayed and coated as much as other oranges and they will therefore not keep so well, so if you don't freeze them they need to be used quite quickly.

Muslin bags or squares can be purchased at most cookshops.

I find that this is the only significant use I make of my pressure cooker all year, but it is worth having one just for this.

MAKES ABOUT 2 KG (BETWEEN 4 AND 5 LB)

900 g (2 lb) Seville oranges
1.2 litres (2 pints) water
Juice of 2 lemons
1.8 kg (4 lb) caster or ordinary granulated sugar (warmed slightly in a low oven)

1. Pre-heat the oven to about 130°C (250°F/Gas Mark ½) and put clean jars and lids into it. This both sterilises them and ensures a good seal when they cool down.

2. Wash and scrub the fruit. Halve it. Squeeze out the juice and keep the pips and any other gunge which comes out while you squeeze. Cut the peel in quarters and scrape the pieces of peel to remove the white pith (it is easier to do this with a quarter orange than a half orange). Put the pith and pips in a muslin bag and tie loosely.

3. Put half the water, the orange and lemon juice, the peel and the bag of pips in a pressure cooker. Cook for 10 minutes at medium pressure and allow the pressure to reduce at room temperature.

4. Lift out the bag of pips. Squeeze it well keeping the juice that comes out of it. This is the procedure which extracts the pectin which is necessary for setting the marmalade, so you will notice that what comes out of the bag is quite viscous. Strain the fruit putting the juice pack into the pan with the other half of the water.

5. Shred the peel, as thickly or finely as you like. (I take each quarter individually and cut into thin strips with a kitchen knife, getting perhaps 12–15 slices from each quarter.) Put back into the pan.

6. Bring to the boil in the open pan on a high heat, add the warmed sugar and then stir over a low heat until entirely dissolved. Then boil again as rapidly as possible until setting point is reached.

7. Lift the pan from the heat, leave for a few minutes until a skin forms (otherwise the peel will rise in the jars) and fill the pre-warmed jars to the top. Put lids on straight away and label with the date and batch number before you forget.

Note on setting point: Boiling may be necessary from anything from 5 to 20 minutes. I did not believe this before I found it to be true from experience. I suspect that it is due to different oranges having varying amounts of pectin or juice in them – or possibly to the efficiency with which we have extracted the pectin. We have found that setting point is most easily tested by dipping in a wooden spoon, lifting it and turning it two or three times and then watching the marmalade dripping from the edge. If the last drop does not drip but stays as a blob of jelly, setting point has been reached. The shorter the boiling time, the lighter the colour and fruitier the taste of the marmalade will be. Marmalade boiled for two hours will be very dark in colour and taste mainly of toffee.

FEBRUARY

Not Valentine's night dinner
(I leave it to you to work out why)

Celeriac, haricot bean and roast garlic soup

Roast: artichokes, parsnips, butternut squash, shallots and garlic
potatoes with a tomato, saffron and almond sauce

Rhubarb and blood orange panettone pudding

Valentine's night dinner – the real McCoy

Champagne cocktail

Chicory and butternut squash pancakes
with a Gruyère and white wine sauce

White chocolate physalis

Tokaji with cantuccini

Seasonal pleasure: chocolate

*(seasonal because large doses of chocolate are
required to maintain health and happiness in February)*

Dorothy Goodbody's chocolate cake with chocolate sauce

Chocolate and rosemary pot

Jurgen Quick's iced chocolate terrine with brandy crème anglaise

Chocolate and marmalade tart

Not Valentine's night dinner

CELERIAC, HARICOT BEAN AND ROAST GARLIC SOUP

This is a surprisingly rich and creamy soup, despite its humble ingredients. The haricot beans and roast garlic make an excellent base for all sorts of winter vegetables (e.g. parsnips and turnips), but celeriac is my favourite partner.

I find that most pulses require either some citrus juice, vinegar or strong spices to redeem their blandness, but if you like a more mellow flavour use less lemon juice. I had some complaints from people who enjoyed cooking from my first book, but found some of the lemon and lime flavours too sharp. Be warned – I like lemons and limes!

SERVES 6–8

150 g (5 oz) dried haricot beans, soaked overnight and then drained
1.5 litres (2¾ pints) water
2 bulbs garlic
800 g (1 lb) celeriac, roughly diced
3 tbsp sunflower oil
Juice of one lemon

1. Put the haricot beans and water in a large pan. Bring to the boil, boil fiercely for 10 minutes then cover and continue to simmer until the haricot beans are quite tender. You are going to purée this soup so it doesn't matter if they are a little overcooked.

2. Meanwhile pre-heat the oven to 190°C (375°F/Gas Mark 5). Put the two whole bulbs of garlic (i.e. about 20 cloves of garlic) on to a small baking sheet and cover with foil. Bake for about 30 minutes until there is some

'give' when the garlic is pressed, but it is not completely squishy. Allow the garlic to cool then cut the top off the whole clove and carefully squeeze out the cooked insides. If this doesn't seem to be working you can simply peel the garlic but that takes longer.

3. In a covered heavy-bottomed pan, sweat the celeriac in the sunflower oil until it is quite tender (about 30 minutes). Do not rush this part or the soup will not be as smooth as it should be.

4. Add the haricot beans and their cooking liquor, the roast garlic and the lemon juice to the celeriac. Blend thoroughly, adding more water if necessary to achieve the correct consistency. Taste and serve. You can garnish the soup with finely chopped parsley, either flat or curly-leaf. Parsley goes particularly well with garlic.

ROAST: ARTICHOKES, PARSNIPS, BUTTERNUT SQUASH, SHALLOTS AND GARLIC POTATOES WITH A TOMATO, SAFFRON AND ALMOND SAUCE

This is basically an excuse for eating lots of roast winter vegetables with some posh tomato ketchup. However, it can be presented in quite an elegant way and is dairy-free. You can vary the vegetables according to what is available, but be sure to include potatoes.

The only tricky thing is to cook all the vegetables correctly – don't just bung them together on a tray or some will be overdone and some will be under-done. And it's not just a question of the cooking time. Part of the process of roasting vegetables is that the oven air drives out some of their moisture (hence crisp skins), and this won't happen if too many vegetables are crowded together on a tray. The timings for the vegetables are of necessity imprecise since vegetables roast much more quickly in large, empty ovens (and of course even more quickly if they are fan-assisted) than in full ovens with lots of moisture in the air. This recipe demands a lot of baking sheets and a lot of space in the oven.

The sauce can be made in advance and reheated, but it tends to thicken up as it stands so you may want to add a bit more water and re-check the season-ing before serving.

The sauce

3 tbsp olive oil
2 cloves garlic, crushed
150 g (6 oz) onion, finely chopped
300 ml (10 fl oz) white wine
1 x 400g (14 oz) tin plum tomatoes
0.1 g (good pinch) saffron strands (saffron often comes in 0.2g sachets)
1 tsp molasses sugar

40 g (1½ oz) ground almonds
25 g (1 oz) breadcrumbs

1. Warm the olive oil in a saucepan. Add the crushed garlic and fry until the garlic has browned but not burned – you are looking for the very particular taste of well-fried garlic in this sauce. Add the onion and continue to cook until the onion is soft. Add the wine, tomatoes, saffron and sugar. Bring to the boil and simmer for about 30 minutes on a very low heat.

2. Toast the ground almonds until they are golden, either in the oven or in a dry frying pan. Repeat this process with the breadcrumbs.

3. When the tomato mixture has simmered for long enough, take it off the heat and add the ground almonds and toasted breadcrumbs. Blend thoroughly with a stick blender or in a food processor. Check the seasoning and texture. Add a little water if necessary. If you are preparing the sauce ahead of time, you may need to add some more water when you re-heat it, as the breadcrumbs and almonds make it thicken up over time.

The vegetables

400 g (14 oz) large potatoes
3 tbsp sunflower oil
1 clove garlic, crushed
1 red chilli (with seeds), very finely chopped
1 tsp paprika

450 g (1 lb) parsnips
2 tbsp sunflower oil

300 g (10 oz) shallots
1 tbsp olive oil

400 g (14 oz) butternut squash
2 tbsp olive oil

300 g (10 oz) Jerusalem artichokes
1 tbsp sunflower oil

Half a medium-sized Savoy cabbage, finely sliced

1. Pre-heat the oven to 230°C (450°F/Gas Mark 8).

2. Prepare all the vegetables. The parsnips should be peeled and halved. If they are very large and woody, quarter them and take out the woody core of each quarter. The potatoes should be thoroughly washed (I prefer them unpeeled) and cut into wedges, probably about 6 from a typical baking-sized potato. The shallots should be peeled – if they are very large, like the temptingly-named banana shallots, they can be cut into four lengthways. The squash should be cut into long fat strips, retaining the shape of the vegetable. It is slightly nicer peeled, but this is by no means essential. The artichokes should be thoroughly cleaned and cut in half if they are large.

3. Put the potato wedges into a good-sized pan of water and put it on to boil. After it comes to the boil simmer for a further 5–10 minutes until the potatoes are just beginning to go feathery at the edges, but are not

quite cooked. Take the potatoes out with a slotted spoon, retaining the water, and turn gently in the sunflower oil with plenty of salt and pepper. Spread out onto a baking sheet and place in the pre-heated oven for 30–50 minutes until golden on the outside and fluffy within. The potatoes will need turning over ⅔ of the way through the cooking time when their bottoms are cooked. Before you turn them over combine the garlic, chilli and paprika. Coat the potatoes with the mixture as you turn them over – if you add all this at the beginning the garlic will burn.

4. The parsnips can be put in the potato water when you take the potatoes out. Don't blanch the two vegetables together, because the parsnips cook more quickly. Bring the parsnips back to the boil and simmer until just tender – about five minutes. Drain and toss in sunflower oil and salt and pepper and put in the oven for about 25 minutes, turning after 15 minutes, until golden all over.

5. The shallots, squash and artichokes do not need to be blanched before roasting. Simply toss each vegetable in the oil with some salt, spread out on separate baking sheets and put in the oven. The shallots will take about 25 minutes until tender on the inside and sweet and browned on the outside. Both the squash and artichokes will be a little quicker than this. The squash should be browning in places and very soft; the artichokes should be tender.

6. When all the vegetables are nearly ready, re-heat the sauce (thinning with a little water if necessary) and put a large pan of water on to boil. Put the cabbage in the boiling water, bring back to the boil and boil fiercely for about a minute. Drain thoroughly and toss in olive oil, salt and pepper.

7. To serve elegantly, spread a ladleful of sauce on each person's plate. Make a little heap of cabbage in the centre of the plate and put the shallots and artichoke on top (divided evenly between each plate). Then make spokes of a wheel with the rest of the vegetables which should all be more or less long and thin in shape. Serve at once.

RHUBARB AND BLOOD ORANGE PANETTONE PUDDING

If you are lucky you may find Italian delis selling off panettone left over from Christmas. They make a delicious bread and butter pudding. If you can't find any fresh rhubarb this early you can substitute rhubarb jam – in which case you don't need the first lot of sugar.

SERVES 6

½ panettone, broken into biggish pieces
(or a small white uncut loaf if you can't find any panettone)
250 g (8 oz) butter unsalted, melted
300 g (12 oz) rhubarb
100 g (4 oz) light muscovado sugar
3 blood oranges (or good ordinary oranges if you can't find blood oranges)

3 eggs
100 g (4 oz) light muscovado sugar
150 ml (5 fl oz) single cream
2 tbsp demerara sugar

1. Break up the panettone into rough chunks (about 3 cm/1½ inches square) and put into a medium baking dish, about 30 cm x 20 cm (12 inches x 8 inches).

2. Melt the butter and pour evenly over the panettone, allowing it to soak in.

3. Make the rhubarb pulp by placing the rhubarb in a saucepan with the first lot of light muscovado sugar and cooking with the lid on until the rhubarb has released all of its own juice (about 15 minutes). Remove the lid and allow the contents to reduce until the mixture becomes sticky and resembles a soft and sticky jam.

4. Add the blood oranges to the rhubarb pulp and spoon the mixture over the panettone. Allow it to soak in.

5. In a bowl, mix together the eggs, the second lot of light muscovado sugar and single cream to make the custard.

6. Pour the custard over the panettone mixture.

7. Spoon the demerara sugar evenly over the custard and bake at 180°C (350°F) for about 40 minutes, or until just set. It's best eaten while still warm, but is also delicious (although different) cold the next day.

Valentine's night dinner

The only bit of this meal which requires any cooking to speak of is the main course – and most of that can be done the day before, leaving plenty of time for doing whatever else needs to be done on Valentine's night!

Champagne cocktail

A champagne cocktail is the most delicious way to get a slug of alcohol into your veins quickly. Put a lump of sugar in the bottom of each glass, over which you pour a measure of brandy. Top the glass up with champagne.

White chocolate physalis

To make the chocolate physalises (also known as Cape gooseberries), melt some white chocolate in a bowl set over some simmering water. Peel back but don't remove the feathery leaves of the physalis and dunk the fruit in melted white chocolate, holding it by the stalk. Place the coated fruit on a plate which has been very generously dusted with icing sugar and chill thoroughly.

Tokaji with cantuccini

Tokaji is a delicious sweet wine from Hungary and is my favourite substitute for vin santo, the Italian sweet wine to be used if you want to be authentic. Pour a couple of glasses and then dunk cantuccini (very hard nutty biscuits available from Italian delis). A really good and simple finish to a meal.

CHICORY AND BUTTERNUT SQUASH PANCAKES WITH A GRUYÈRE AND WHITE WINE SAUCE

This is a dish you can prepare the day before and then stick in the oven whilst romantically sipping your champagne cocktail. Serve it either with a green salad, or some blanched Savoy cabbage tossed in seasoned olive oil or some really rich and slow-cooked red cabbage (see *Food from The Place Below* for recipe).

There are endless possible variations on the theme of stuffed pancakes with a cheese sauce. I think that braised chicory is a particularly good component as its bitterness complements the rich sweetness of the cheese sauce. Thinly sliced blanched celeriac or Jerusalem artichokes would be other good winter possibilities. You can also vary the cheese – smoked cheddar or Stilton work well with the latter two variations.

Pancakes

*(makes about a dozen pancakes of the size you want –
freeze those you don't want to use in the next day or so)*

125 g (4 oz) plain flour
Pinch of salt
1 egg
300 ml (10 fl oz) milk
Sunflower oil for frying

FOR THE FILLING AND SAUCE
FOR 2 PEOPLE:

2 good-sized heads of chicory
1 tbsp olive oil
1 scant tsp caster sugar

250 g (9 oz) butternut squash, sliced thinly, like packet cheese slices
1 tbsp olive oil

20 g (1 oz) butter
1 good tbsp plain white flour
100 ml (4 fl oz) white wine
100 ml (4 fl oz) cream
100 ml (4 fl oz) milk

125 g (4 oz) Gruyère cheese, grated
(proper Gruyère or Comte cut from a large wheel,
not the dreadful stuff that comes off a square block)

1. Pre-heat the oven to 220°C (425°F/Gas Mark 7).

2. First make the pancakes. Whizz all the pancake ingredients in a blender
   and leave to stand for a few minutes. Heat a little oil in a good pancake
   pan (I use one about 6 inches in diameter) until it is smoking. Add a
   small ladleful of batter and move it around so the bottom of the pan is
   evenly coated. Ease the edges of the pancake with a spatula and when the
   first side is done, flip it over and briefly cook the other side. Stack cooked
   pancakes on a plate – there is no need to keep them warm.

3. Next roast the vegetables. Halve the chicory lengthways, toss in the oil,
   sugar and a little salt and put in a small roasting tray covered with foil and
   put in the oven.

4. Toss the squash in the olive oil and some salt and put on an uncovered
   roasting tray in the oven.

5. After about 20 minutes turn the pieces of squash over. After about another 10 minutes they should be coloured on both sides and quite tender. Remove the squash from the oven. By about this time the chicory should be tender but rather wet. Remove the foil covering and leave in the oven for another quarter of an hour or so and then take out of the oven.

6. Next stuff the pancakes. Put a pancake flat on a plate or work surface and put one piece of chicory (i.e. half a chicory head) on it. Add a couple of pieces of squash and a sprinkling of Gruyère. Roll up the pancake and put it in a small buttered gratin dish. Repeat with a further three pancakes, using up all the roast vegetables in the process, arranging them side by side.

7. Make the cheese sauce. Melt the butter in a saucepan and sprinkle the flour on. Stir the flour in to make a roux. Add the wine a little at a time, stirring vigorously between each addition. In a separate pan, heat the milk until almost boiling. Gradually add the milk to the sauce, making sure each addition is fully incorporated before adding the next bit. When all the milk is added bring the sauce to the boil and simmer for a few minutes, then take off the heat. Add the cream and cheese. Taste the sauce — you may well not want to add any salt, as there is quite a lot of cheese.

8. Pour the sauce over the pancakes and sprinkle the remaining cheese on top (stop at this point if you are preparing the night before). Put back in the oven for about 25 minutes until bubbling on top. You can serve at once, but it won't be a disaster if you want to leave it standing for half an hour or so.

Seasonal pleasure: chocolate

DOROTHY GOODBODY'S CHOCOLATE CAKE WITH CHOCOLATE SAUCE

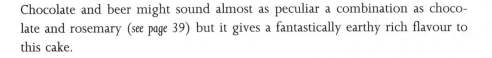

Chocolate and beer might sound almost as peculiar a combination as chocolate and rosemary (*see page 39*) but it gives a fantastically earthy rich flavour to this cake.

In London we use Samuel Smith's oatmeal stout. In Hereford we use Dorothy Goodbody's stout from the excellent Wye Valley Brewery. Dorothy is a voluptuous invention of Pete Amor (whose brewery it is) and tales of her adventures (Dorothy Catches Crabs, Enter Dorothy Goodbody, Dorothy's Big Bang) are told at Wye Valley beer festivals and even during the much more salubrious Three Choirs Festival.

125 g (4 oz) unsalted butter
275 g (9 oz) dark soft brown sugar
2 eggs
170 g (6 oz) plain flour
½ tsp baking powder
1 tsp bicarbonate of soda
200 ml (7 fl oz) Dorothy Goodbody's stout or similar dark beer
75 g (3 oz) cocoa powder

1. Preheat the oven to 180°C (350°F/Gas Mark 4).

2. Line a 19 cm (7½ inch) springform tin.

3. Cream the butter and sugar together.

4. Add the eggs gradually and beat until pale and fluffy.

5. Sift flour and bicarbonate and baking powder.

6. In another bowl slowly mix the beer into the cocoa.

7. Alternately add cocoa mix and flour mix to the butter/sugar/eggs in small quantities.

8. Bake for about one hour until a skewer inserted into the middle comes out clean.

9. Leave to cool. If you are not going to eat it immediately either clingfilm the cake once it has cooled, or store in an airtight tin.

10. Serve with warm Chocolate Sauce (*below*) or with Brandy Crème Anglaise (*see page 41*).

Chocolate sauce

150 g (6 oz) chocolate
250 ml (10 fl oz) double cream

1. Warm the chocolate and cream slowly together in a heavy-bottomed pan on a medium heat.

2. Take off the heat before the chocolate has quite finished melting. Stir to a silky smoothness. The sauce is ready to serve now or can be re-heated subsequently.

CHOCOLATE AND ROSEMARY POT

For my 30th birthday Sarah took me on a surprise trip to the wonderful Peat Inn in Fife, Scotland. I gorged myself on a dessert with the unexpected but delicious combination of chocolate and rosemary. This is our version. Although the quantities look small, it is rich enough to mean that this should be enough for at least six people.

SERVES 6

25 g (1 oz) caster sugar
180 ml (6 fl oz) white wine
Juice of half a lemon
600 ml (1 pint) double cream
2 sprigs fresh rosemary
225 g (8 oz) best quality dark chocolate, broken into chunks

1. Warm the sugar, wine and lemon juice in a pan – don't use an aluminium pan for this as this mixture is rather acidic. Stir until the sugar has dissolved.

2. Stir in the cream; the mixture will thicken. Add the rosemary and the chocolate and stir until it has melted.

3. Bring to the boil. Turn down and simmer gently for 25–35 minutes or until the mixture is dark and thick. If the mixture separates, allow to cool and whizz it in a blender.

4. Leave to cool slightly (but not to set) and strain into six ramekins. Allow to cool for several hours in the fridge until set. Garnish with a little sprig of rosemary dusted with icing sugar on each one.

JURGEN QUICK'S ICED CHOCOLATE TERRINE

It may seem strange to have an iced recipe as an ideal winter pudding, but this is so rich and full of chocolate that it fortifies you well enough to face the coldest, wettest week – especially if the terrine is served with a brandy-enriched crème anglaise. This recipe was given to us by Jurgen, our first chef for our evening dinners at The Place Below, who gave me a whole new vision of the rich and delicious possibilities of a posher style of vegetarian food.

SERVES 8

75 g (3 oz) dark cooking chocolate
6 egg yolks
120 g (4 oz) caster sugar
2 tbsp strong black coffee
50 g (2 oz) clear honey
120 g (4 oz) unsalted butter, at room temperature
65 g (2½ oz) cocoa powder
300 ml (10 fl oz) double cream

1. Line a 900 g (2 lb) loaf tin with clingfilm and set aside.

2. Break the chocolate into small chunks and melt directly over a low heat in a heavy-bottomed pan, stirring constantly, or in a bowl set over a pan of gently simmering water or in a microwave. I find a microwave or direct heat best – fiddling around with bowls on pans makes me impatient. Remove from the heat and stir in the egg yolks, sugar, coffee and honey.

3. Beat the butter in a bowl until creamy – you can do this by hand or using a food processor or a hand-held beater. Add the cocoa powder and stir into the chocolate mixture.

4. Whip the double cream until it just holds it shape and then fold into the chocolate mixture until evenly combined. Pour into the lined tin and freeze until solid for about 8 hours or overnight.

5. To serve, invert the tin over a board and ease out the terrine by carefully pulling the excess clingfilm. (If it is stuck you can put the bottom of the tin briefly into a sink of hot water to loosen it.) Peel the film away from the terrine and cut into generous slices. Serve with either Brandy Crème Anglaise (*see below*) or single cream.

Brandy crème anglaise

Cold custard doesn't sound very nice whereas 'brandy crème anglaise' really sounds quite enticing.

SERVES 8

300 ml (10 fl oz) *whole milk*
1 tsp *vanilla essence*
4 *egg yolks*
25 g (1 oz) *caster sugar*
1 tbsp *brandy*

1. Heat the milk and vanilla essence in a small saucepan until almost boiling. Remove from the heat.

2. Whisk the egg yolks with the sugar in a bowl until the mixture is pale and creamy. Beat in the warm milk. Return to the pan.

3. Place over a low heat and stir for about 5–10 minutes until it thickens a little. Whisk in the brandy. Leave to cool and then taste to see if it needs some more brandy. Serve cold with slices of the Iced Chocolate Terrine or with the Chocolate and Marmalade Tart or with Dorothy Goodbody's Chocolate Cake (*see pages 40, 42 and 37*).

CHOCOLATE AND MARMALADE TART

This is basically a repeat of the chocolate and prune tart in *Food from The Place Below*, but it is such a good variation that I think it is worth giving the recipe again in full. It's an adult version of Jaffa Cakes or Terry's Chocolate Orange.

This tart is best served with crème fraîche, which is best bought from Neal's Yard Dairy on Dorstone Hill near Hereford about four miles from where I'm writing this. However, full fat crème fraîche of any sort will do perfectly well.

SERVES 8

100 g (4 oz) unsalted butter
100 g (4 oz) good quality plain chocolate
1 egg
3 egg yolks
25 g (1 oz) caster sugar

1 x 23 cm (9 inch) *Sweet Pastry Case*, baked blind (see page x)

200 g (7 oz) marmalade (preferably Uncle Tony's – see page 19)

1. Pre-heat the oven to 190°C (375°F/Gas Mark 5).

2. Melt the butter in a pan over a low heat. Break the chocolate up a bit and melt it into the butter. Remove from the heat.

3. In a bowl, whisk the egg and egg yolks with the sugar until the mixture will leave a trail when the whisk is lifted. Fold it into the chocolate and butter mix.

4. Spread the marmalade evenly over the bottom of the pastry case. Then spread the chocolate mixture evenly on top of it. Bake in the pre-heated oven for 15 minutes. There should be a thin crust on top, but the mixture should still be mousse-like underneath. Delicious served either still slightly warm or thoroughly chilled, in either case with a good dollop of crème fraîche.

MARCH

March is a month which occasionally hints at spring,
but is often closer to winter.

Shrove Tuesday dinner

Warm salad of chicory, roast sweet potato and Cashel Blue

Charred aubergine and buffalo mozzarella blini with
Italian wild rocket

Buttered beetroot and blood oranges

Christopher Lloyd's rhubarb and lemon tart
Or (if it really is Shrove Tuesday) pancakes with lemon and sugar

Still winter supper

Sweet potato, fennel and Caerphilly pie and stir-fried
kale with cumin and lemon

Banoffee pie

Seasonal pleasures: four serious soups to cheer up Lenten days

Fennel and green pea soup with parsley and lemon

Parsnip, Cheddar and rosemary soup

Leek and potato soup with Thai flavours

Rich sweet potato and lentil soup

Shrove Tuesday dinner

Shrove Tuesday is, of course, the day for clearing the larder of all rich and delicious things such as eggs and oil before the beginning of Lent. As a result, the tradition of eating pancakes has developed. Well, it's as good an excuse as any. If you want to do a pancake recipe but the blinis are not to your taste, then try the Valentine's night pancake recipe. Or if you want to serve two courses of pancakes, use the pancake mix recipe given on the Valentine's night recipe (*see page 34*) and simply serve it with lemon juice and sugar (or maple syrup, or home made jam) for pudding.

WARM SALAD OF CHICORY, ROAST SWEET POTATO AND CASHEL BLUE

I've felt a little bit ambivalent about chicory until recently, but I'm now a convert. It wants to be served with things which are rich and sweet to contrast with its natural bitterness. The creamy ripeness of Cashel Blue is perfect for this salad. Dolcelatte would be an acceptable substitute. If you were to use Beenleigh Blue or Roquefort you would probably want to use a smaller quantity of cheese.

SERVES 6

9 heads chicory (6 for braising and 3 for the salad)
2 tbsp olive oil
1 tsp caster sugar
3 medium-sized orange-fleshed sweet potatoes
(about 750 g/1 lb 10 oz), cut into six long wedges each
2 tbsp olive oil

50 g (2 oz) rocket
2 tbsp walnut oil
½ tbsp balsamic vinegar
Salt and freshly ground black pepper
150 g Cashel Blue, cut into thin strips

1. Pre-heat the oven to 220°C (425°F/Gas Mark 7).

2. Halve six of the chicory heads lengthways and toss them in the first lot of olive oil, the sugar and some salt. Put on a baking tray and cover with foil. Put in the oven for 30 minutes. Take off the foil; the chicory should be tender by now. Return to the oven for a further 15 minutes to dry it out a little. Then take out and set aside.

3. Turn the sweet potato wedges in the remaining olive oil and some salt and put on a baking sheet, skin sides down. Put in the oven for 30–40 minutes until very tender and colouring in patches. Set aside.

4. If you have cooked the chicory and sweet potatoes ahead of time (which is fine) they want to go back into the oven for 10–15 minutes to warm up before serving.

5. Break up the remaining chicory heads and mix with the rocket, walnut oil and balsamic vinegar. Season with salt and freshly ground black pepper and toss thoroughly.

6. Divide the salad between six plates. Arrange the warm vegetables on top of and around the leaves and put the little strips of Cashel Blue on top of the vegetables.

CHARRED AUBERGINE AND BUFFALO MOZZARELLA BLINI, BEETROOT WITH BUTTER AND ORANGES, ITALIAN WILD ROCKET

※

This is a kind of pizza pancake. I got the idea of using charred aubergine after we had a big phase of making Baba Ganoush (*see page* 127) at The Place Below. If you have not used this method of cooking aubergines before it would be worth reading the notes on page 127 before trying this recipe. The pungency of the smoky aubergine and the salty sun-dried tomatoes go beautifully with the rich smoothness of just-melted mozzarella.

People who haven't been to southern Italy are sometimes sceptical that proper mozzarella is really made from buffalo milk; but as you drive south from Naples you will see this wonderful sight of herd after herd of buffaloes, and signs everywhere advertising the local cheese. If you can get hold of really fresh buffalo mozzarella, you will taste the difference. At one stage we had a supplier who told us that the buffalo were milked on Wednesday morning, the cheese made on Wednesday evening and the cheese was flown over on Thursday and delivered to The Place Below on Thursday lunchtime. I'm a great sucker for stories like that – and it was certainly the most delicious cheese.

Blinis are traditionally made with buckwheat flour. This recipe is a lighter and fluffier alternative. They can be made the day before, stacked and wrapped in clingfilm – although they will be nicer if you make them just before using them. Mini versions can be used for making delicious canapés.

1 x 7 g sachet easy blend yeast
250 ml (9 fl oz) warm milk
125 ml (4 fl oz) warm water
140 g (5 oz) plain white flour
3 medium eggs, separated
½ tsp salt
Pinch sugar
Sunflower oil for frying

2 large aubergines (about 700 g – 900 g/1½ – 2 lb)
40 g (1½ oz) sun-dried tomatoes, soaked for about 1 hour in hot water and drained
(or 85 g (3 oz) sun-dried tomatoes in oil), very finely chopped
1 tsp balsamic vinegar
3 tbsp olive oil
Handful fresh basil leaves, torn into small pieces
1 clove garlic, crushed
2 buffalo mozzarella balls (about 140 g/5 oz each), roughly chopped

1. To make the blinis, place the yeast, milk, water, flour, egg yolks, salt and sugar in a blender or food processor. Process for about a minute until completely smooth. Pour into a mixing bowl and cover with plastic film. Leave to rise for 1½ to 2 hours.

2. Once risen, whip the egg whites until they are stiff and fold into the batter.

3. Brush a small amount of oil on the bottom of a frying pan and heat. Make one blini at a time using either a 50 ml ladleful (to make 12 blinis) or a 100 ml ladleful (to make 6 larger blinis). Cook for 2 minutes until golden brown. Place on a plate and set aside. Continue making the blinis until all the mixture is used up.

4. To make the blini topping, put the whole aubergines onto an open gas flame, or under a fierce grill until the skin is charred all over and the flesh has collapsed. The open gas flame method produces the best result and is very quick but is a little scary the first time you do it (see note on page 127). Allow to cool then peel carefully, trying to waste as little of the flesh as possible.

5. Chop the aubergine flesh roughly and mix with all the remaining ingredients except the mozzarella. Season to taste.

6. Pre-heat the oven to 200°C (400°F/Gas Mark 6). Place the cooked pancakes on two large baking sheets. Divide the aubergine mix between them and spread evenly, leaving a small gap around the edges. Divide the chopped buffalo mozzarella between the pancakes. Bake for about 10 minutes until the cheese is just beginning to melt. Serve at once with the Buttered Beetroot and Blood Oranges (*see page* 52) and some spicy greens, such as rocket.

BUTTERED BEETROOT
AND BLOOD ORANGES

The best way to cook beetroot is to bake it, a method followed with all beet-root recipes in this book. If you don't have time to do this and you intend to buy ready-cooked beetroot (which will have been boiled), make sure that it hasn't been stored in vinegar or it will be completely useless for this recipe, which requires plainly cooked beetroot. In fact I think beetroot stored in vinegar is a vicious thing, not only because it tastes horrible, but also because it has made millions of people think they don't like beetroot, which in reality has the mildest and most delicate of flavours. Beetroot does go well with acidic flavours (oranges and a little balsamic vinegar in this recipe, or classi-cally sour cream) but sousing in malt vinegar does a delicious and beautiful vegetable no favours at all.

If you can get blood oranges (they should be available at least in early March) they are particularly good, but decent ordinary oranges also work perfectly well.

SERVES 6

40 g (2 oz) butter
500 g (1 lb) beetroot, baked the day before until tender (see page 198 for
further instructions), peeled and cut into 2 cm (1 inch) cubes
1 tsp balsamic vinegar
2 large blood oranges, peeled and segmented

1. Heat the butter in a large frying pan. Add the cubed beetroot and cook gently for about 5–10 minutes until the beetroot is heated through.

2. Add the balsamic vinegar and stir well. Remove from the heat and gently stir in the orange segments. Serve at once.

Rhubarb

You will notice from these March recipes that rhubarb is something that I like a lot. This is because it has an assertive and individual flavour, it is cheap (apart from very early in the year), and it is only available in season.

It is at its most tender and sweetest early in the year. The Yorkshire rhubarb specialists will have blanched rhubarb in the shops as early as January, a month when rhubarb festivals and competitions take place in that county. What was once a prized seasonal (and regional) delicacy at a time of year when there was a paucity of fruit is now competing with crunchy strawberries and bruised but unripe mangoes for our attention on the supermarket shelves. Why not wait for the British strawberry season and the Indian Alfonso mango season, and stick with early rhubarb and pears in January? If you grow rhubarb yourself it is more likely to be ready for a first picking in March.

CHRISTOPHER LLOYD'S
RHUBARB AND LEMON TART

For anyone like me, setting out on the business of growing vegetables, but with a primary interest in food rather than gardening, Christopher Lloyd's *Gardener Cook* (Frances Lincoln, 1997) is a fantastic book. There are lots of highly delicious, straightforward recipes and comments about preparing particular fruits and vegetables, combined with helpful comments about which varieties to grow, when to plant them etc. Whereas most cookbooks that I like get stained with food, my copy of *Gardener Cook* has been trashed by excessive exposure to wind and rain as well (actually three rainy days and nights in the veg plot after an exhausting bean-planting session).

This is a lovely simple recipe, which we've started serving regularly at the Café @ All Saints. It is one you really want to eat within a few hours of making it.

SERVES 8 GENEROUSLY

125 g (4 oz) light muscovado sugar
200 ml (7 fl oz) water

1 kg (2 lb) rhubarb, cut into 3 cm (1¼ inch) pieces

4 egg yolks
125 g (4 oz) caster sugar
150 ml (5 fl oz) double cream
Finely grated zest of one lemon

1 blind-baked 23 cm (9 inch) Sweet Pastry Shell (see page x)

1. Pre-heat the oven to 190°C (375°F/Gas Mark 5).

2. Stir the sugar and water together over a medium heat until the sugar dissolves, then bring to a light boil. Add the chopped rhubarb and simmer for one minute – don't let the fruit go mushy. Drain and reserve the rhubarb.

3. Beat the egg yolks and sugar in a bowl with an electric beater until they are voluminous, white and fluffy – this will take about 3 minutes. Mix in the lemon zest and cream.

4. Spread the rhubarb on the bottom of the tart, cover with the lemon cream filling and bake for 25–30 minutes until the cream filling is lightly browned. Leave for about one hour before serving.

5. To serve, sprinkle with some icing or caster sugar.

Still winter supper

SWEET POTATO, FENNEL AND CAERPHILLY PIE AND STIR-FRIED KALE WITH CUMIN AND LEMON

This is a rich winter pie for which you need a decent winter appetite. Like most things it will taste much better if made with decent ingredients – in this case flavoursome mature Caerphilly. Good mature Lancashire is better than bad Caerphilly.

You can buy OK puff pastry; I'm afraid life is too short to make your own puff pastry at home.

SERVES 4

2 tbsp olive oil
300 g (10 oz) fennel, coarsely chopped
400 g (14 oz) orange-fleshed sweet potatoes, diced (no need to peel)
1 clove garlic, crushed
1 sprig rosemary, stripped from the stalk or 1 scant tsp dried rosemary
Salt and pepper
100 ml (4 fl oz) cider
100 ml (4 fl oz) double cream
125 g (4 oz) mature Caerphilly, grated

1 sheet puff pastry (approx. 300 g/10 oz)
1 egg, lightly beaten for glazing

1. In a heavy-bottomed pan, sweat the fennel, diced sweet potato, garlic and rosemary in the olive oil until the sweet potato is just becoming tender. You need to do this on a high heat but with the lid on stirring regularly

or it will catch. Add some salt part way through to help the sweet potato and fennel become tender.

2. When the sweet potato is just tender add the cider. Bubble fiercely for a couple of minutes. Add the cream and bubble fiercely for a couple more minutes until there is a thick creamy goo surrounding the fennel and sweet potato. Turn off the heat.

3. Once the mixture has cooled for a couple of minutes stir in the grated cheese and taste. Add salt and pepper as necessary.

4. Put the filling into a baking dish. Roll out the pastry and put on top, crimping the edges and glazing with a little beaten egg. Bake at 230°C (450°F/Gas Mark 8) until the pastry is golden. Serve with the Stir-fried Curly Kale with Cumin and Lemon (*see below*).

Stir-fried curly kale with cumin and lemon

Kale has a strong cabbagey taste which marries well with hefty spicing. This dish has the power needed to cut through the rich creaminess of the Sweet Potato Pie (*see page 56*).

SERVES 4

1 tsp cumin seeds
1 tbsp sunflower oil
200 g (7 oz) curly kale, finely shredded
Juice of half a good sized lemon
Salt and pepper

1. In a wok, dry-fry the cumin seeds until they are just beginning to turn colour.

2. Add the oil and then the kale. Stir-fry until the kale is tender (about 5 minutes).

3. Add the lemon juice and some salt and pepper to taste. Toss together and serve.

BANOFFEE PIE

I was always very doubtful about banoffee pie. It was a silly name, without any interesting ingredients, fit only to be puréed and fed to small children. Well, I'm now a complete convert. This is a version which Frances Tomlinson brought along to The Place Below and is utterly yummy. I think that the key is to use a generous quantity of thoroughly cooked condensed milk. Our queen of tarts in Hereford, Mel Brown, has created more happiness with this recipe than almost anything else we make at the Café @ All Saints.

The Nestlé cans (the most commonly available brand of sweetened condensed milk) carry a warning that they should not be boiled or there is a danger that they will explode. We have never had this experience, but risk-avoiders may wish to follow Nestlé's advice and not make this recipe in this way. We always heat the cans in a large pan full of (initially) cold water which we then bring slowly to the boil and then simmer gently for about three hours. Be very careful that there is always plenty of water in the pan – if it boils dry that would certainly increase the risk of an explosion. We then allow the unopened cans to cool overnight in the pan of water before opening. Once you have tasted the luxurious soft toffee flavour of condensed milk boiled in this way, all thoughts of explosions and other risks will be banished from your head, and spoon after spoon will be magically transferred to your lips.

Be sure to bake the empty tart shell fully, as the tart gets no further cooking.

1 blind baked 23 cm (9 inch) Sweet Tart Shell (see page x)

400 g (13½ oz) tin condensed milk, boiled the day before (be sure to read the introductory warning paragraph above). For a really indulgent pie you could use one and a half tins, but that leaves you with half a tin of toffeed condensed milk to eat, which might mean that you fail to eat all your Brussels sprouts at the next meal.

1 kg (2 lb) bananas, in 1 cm (½ inch) slices
400 ml (14 fl oz) double cream, whipped
2 tsp caster sugar
Either one espresso coffee or 2 tsp powdered instant coffee

Cocoa powder to sprinkle on top

1. Spread the cooked, condensed milk evenly over the blind-baked sweet tart shell. Arrange the chopped bananas in an even layer on top of this.

2. Whip the cream with the sugar and coffee and then spread it evenly on top. Garnish with a dusting of cocoa powder and chill until you are ready to eat. It is better eaten the day it is made – it is fine for one further day if kept in the fridge, but no longer than that.

Seasonal pleasures: four serious soups to cheer up Lenten days

FENNEL AND GREEN PEA SOUP WITH PARSLEY AND LEMON

Lots of people are put off by the thought of fennel soup, associating it with the strong aniseed taste of raw fennel. Cooked fennel has a much gentler flavour, and as well as being delicious roasted (either in a salad or in a quiche, preferably paired with Gruyère cheese) it is lovely in this simple and well-balanced soup.

Although in the UK we think of raw fennel as a summer vegetable, its traditional time of harvest and usage in Sicily is during the winter. It is after all a 'root' vegetable, but with a more aristocratic image than turnips and swedes.

I think I should repeat at every opportunity in this book that pulses (and potatoes) require generous seasoning.

SERVES 6

125 g (4 oz) split green peas

4 tbsp olive oil
500 g (1 lb) fennel (2 smallish ones)
125 g (4 oz) leek (1 small one)
2 cloves garlic, crushed
50 g (2 oz) parsley (a large supermarket bunch), finely chopped

Juice of half a lemon
Salt and freshly ground black pepper

1. Boil the split green peas in 1.5 litres (2¾ pints) of water until they are mushy (about 45 minutes to an hour). Set on one side and do not drain.

2. In a large lidded pan, sweat the fennel, leek and garlic in the olive oil for about 10 minutes until the fennel is tender but not mushy. Add the split green peas and their cooking liquor and about three quarters of the finely chopped parsley and bring to the boil. Simmer for about 20 minutes with the lid on.

3. Take off the heat, add the lemon, season generously with salt and freshly ground black pepper and purée with a hand-held blender. Check seasoning and garnish each bowl with a little of the reserved parsley.

4. If you have any home-dried tomatoes to hand (*see page 162*), chop them finely and add a few little pieces to each bowl as an additional garnish.

PARSNIP, CHEDDAR AND ROSEMARY SOUP

SERVES 6

2 tbsp olive oil
50 g (2 oz) butter
200 g (7 oz) onions, diced
2 cloves garlic, crushed
2 sticks celery, coarsely chopped
750 g (1½ lb) parsnips, peeled and sliced
1 good sprig rosemary (about 20 leaves), stripped off the stalk

1.5 litres (2¾ pints) water
250 g (8 oz) potatoes, peeled and roughly diced

1 tbsp English mustard
100 g (4 oz) mature Cheddar cheese, grated

1. In a large lidded pan on a medium heat, sweat the onions, garlic, celery and parsnips in the butter and oil with some salt and the rosemary, until they are very soft. This will take at least 20 minutes. It makes all the difference to the smoothness of the final soup if you don't hurry this process, but keep cooking until the parsnips are very soft, stirring well every few minutes.

2. Add the water and potatoes and bring to the boil. Simmer for about 20 minutes until the potatoes are disintegrating.

3. Take off the heat, add the mustard and whizz in a food processor or with a hand-held blender. Add the grated cheese and stir well until it has melted and mixed in with the soup. Season with more salt and freshly ground black pepper and serve.

LEEK AND POTATO SOUP
WITH THAI FLAVOURS

This is a straightforward leek and potato soup with a bit of magic green paste added. The green paste is based on a recipe from the Australian chef Gay Bilson, via South Kensington chef Simon Hopkinson. It is a kind of Asian pesto and we also use a variation of it at both The Place Below and Café @ All Saints to dress a zingy rice noodle salad.

SERVES 6

2 tbsp sunflower oil
500 g (1 lb) leeks, roughly chopped
500 g (1 lb) potatoes, roughly diced

1 large bunch coriander, washed
2 garlic cloves, crushed
1 tsp ground cumin
1 tsp caster sugar
1 tsp salt
Juice of 2 limes (more if they are not very juicy)
1 small green chilli, with seeds (without seeds will be milder)
300 ml (10 fl oz) can coconut milk

A few coriander leaves for garnish

1. Heat the sunflower oil in a large pan and cook the leeks until soft. Add the potatoes and 1.5 litres water (2¾ pints) and bring to the boil. Simmer for about 15 minutes until the potatoes are quite soft.

2. Remove from the heat and stir in all the remaining ingredients. Whizz the soup until it is smooth either in a food processor or (more easily) using a stick blender. Re-heat gently before serving but do not boil. Check the seasoning and thickness – dilute with a little extra water if you like. Garnish each plate with a few coriander leaves.

RICH SWEET POTATO AND LENTIL SOUP

This is very simple and very comforting. But don't make it unless you can get hold of the orange-fleshed variety of sweet potatoes.

You will think that the quantity of olive oil is ridiculously large when you first put it in the pan, but when the soup is finally blended it merges with everything else to create a delicious velvety richness. However, if you like your lentil soups more authentically Lenten, you can cut down on the olive oil.

You will need to add plenty of salt to this soup – lentils and sweet potatoes both need generous seasoning.

SERVES 6–8

100 ml (3½ fl oz) olive oil
375 g (12 oz) onions, roughly chopped
550 g (1 lb 4 oz) orange fleshed sweet potatoes, roughly chopped (no need to peel)
3 cloves garlic, crushed
1 small chilli, finely chopped
2 tsp paprika
250 g (8 oz) red lentils
2 litres (3½ pints) water
2 tbsp balsamic vinegar (not worth using a posh one here)
Salt and freshly ground black pepper

1. Sweat the onions in the olive oil for five minutes. Add the sweet potatoes and continue sweating until they are tender.

2. When they are nearly done add the garlic, chilli and paprika (if you add this at the beginning you will lose most of the garlic flavour) and cook for five more minutes.

3. Add the lentils and water, bring to the boil and simmer until the lentils are quite tender (about 20 minutes). Add the balsamic vinegar and blend thoroughly. Season generously with salt and pepper and serve.

APRIL

Easter lunch

Purple sprouting broccoli, lime hollandaise

Leek and Gruyère brioche with white wine and
tarragon sauce, garlic and chilli roast potatoes,
cauliflower and carrots in a tomato vinaigrette

Rhubarb fool with almond biscuits

Early spring supper

Luke's Cornish cauliflower and coriander soup

Spaghetti with quick pesto, roast potatoes and spring cabbage

Some other quick pasta ideas

Passion fruit syllabub

Seasonal pleasure

The cabbage family (brassicas)

Easter lunch

PURPLE SPROUTING BROCCOLI, LIME HOLLANDAISE

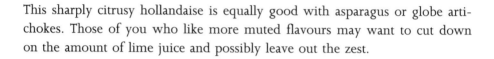

This sharply citrusy hollandaise is equally good with asparagus or globe artichokes. Those of you who like more muted flavours may want to cut down on the amount of lime juice and possibly leave out the zest.

SERVES 6 AS A STARTER

1 kg (2 lb) purple sprouting broccoli

250 g (8 oz) unsalted butter
3 egg yolks
1 dsp cold water
Juice and zest of 1-2 limes
Salt and pepper

1. Prepare the purple sprouting broccoli. Separate the stems from the florets, discarding any floppy or woody bits. Bring a large pan of water to the boil. When the hollandaise is nearly ready (see steps 2–4 below) add the stems and boil for about 3 minutes, add the florets and boil for a further 1–2 minutes until they are just tender. Drain immediately.

2. De-froth (semi-clarify) the butter. Place in a small pan (preferably with a lip) and gently melt. When it has melted, allow to settle for a few minutes, and scoop the froth off with a large spoon. Put the clear butter on the side of the stove to keep warm.

3. This is the tricky bit. Put the three large egg yolks in a pan (not aluminium) and add a good dessertspoonful of cold water. Whisk constantly and vigorously, whipping the pan on and off a low heat. The eggs go through different stages. First, the mixture begins to lighten and become frothy. Shortly after that, the eggs will begin to lose a bit of air and become creamy and pale. The yolks are ready to receive the butter when they are thick enough to retain the distinct marks of the whisk. When they reach that stage, remove from the heat and put on a stable surface (perhaps with a damp cloth underneath to add extra stability).

4. Continue whisking the egg yolks and begin to pour in the warm clear butter, slowly at first and then quicker as the sauce gradually becomes thick and oozy looking. Add a touch of the milky residue from the bottom of the pan to loosen the sauce a little. Then add the lime juice and zest, half at a time in case the full amount is too 'limy' for your taste. Season with salt and pepper to taste. (Purists will insist on white pepper, but I quite like specks of black in this beautiful yellow custard.)

5. This is best served at once. (You can keep the sauce warm for a bit but any attempt to re-warm it risks the sauce splitting.) Divide the drained cooked purple sprouting broccoli between warmed plates and put a big blob of hollandaise on the side of each. No other garnish is necessary for shining Easter eggy perfection.

LEEK AND GRUYÈRE BRIOCHE WITH TARRAGON AND WHITE WINE SAUCE

This is a delicious dish which we have often served at special lunches and dinners at The Place Below, most memorably at the wedding reception for the editor of the *Time Out* eating out guide. The eggy brioche dough makes it particularly suitable for Easter.

MAKES TWO 500 G (1 LB) LOAVES OR ABOUT 8 INDIVIDUAL BRIOCHES

350 g (12 oz) strong white bread flour
50 ml (2 fl oz) milk
1½ tsp salt
1 sachet easy blend yeast (6 g/¼ oz)
4 medium eggs
25 g (1 oz) sugar
200 g (7 oz) butter, softened
1 egg yolk (for glazing)

1. You must start the dough the day before you want to eat the brioche. Put all the ingredients, except the butter and the egg yolk, into the bowl of an electric mixer. Mix briefly with a spoon to make a cohesive but slightly sticky dough, then put the dough hook on and knead on a low speed for 5 minutes.

2. Add one third of the softened butter and continue kneading by machine until the butter has been completely absorbed. Add the next third of the butter and repeat. Repeat once more with the final third of the butter. Once all the butter has been absorbed, continue kneading on a low speed for a further 10 minutes. The dough should be shiny and very soft. If your dough hook does not reach all parts of the bowl efficiently, you may need to stop the machine occasionally to scrape the dough away from those bits of the bowl not being reached. Once the kneading is done, cover the bowl with clingfilm and put in the fridge overnight.

3. The next day, grease the individual brioche tins with butter. Take the dough from the fridge – it may have risen a little, a lot, or not at all, depending on the temperature of the room where you were kneading the day before and the temperature of the fridge. In any event, don't worry if it has not risen – it will do later, as long as the yeast wasn't past its sell-by date. Divide the dough in eight pieces and shape each piece into a roll to fit into one of the tins. (For the traditional appearance, you should separate off a little dough, make little marble-sized spheres and press these into dents in the individual brioches.) Leave to rise until the dough has at least doubled in size – which, be warned, will take 2 to 4 hours.

4. When the brioches look as though they are nearly ready, pre-heat the oven to 220°C (425°F/Gas Mark 7). Brush the top of each loaf with the egg yolk beaten with a little salt, being careful not to get egg yolk on the tins. Bake them for about 25 minutes, until they sound hollow when they are taken out of their tins and tapped on the bottom. Turn the brioches out and leave to cool on a wire rack.

Leek and Gruyère filling

50 g (2 oz) butter
1 kg (2 lb) leeks, trimmed, halved and in 2 cm (1 inch) slices
1 big dsp wholegrain mustard
175 g (6 oz) Gruyère, off the wheel, grated
150 g (5 oz) Greek yoghurt
Salt and pepper

1. Pre-heat the oven to 200°C (400°F/Gas Mark 6). Sweat the leeks in the butter with a little salt until quite tender. Drain very well, reserving the stock for the white sauce.

2. Mix with the remaining ingredients, keeping a little of the cheese separate.

3. Cut off the tops of the cooled brioches. With a small knife, cut around the middles of the brioches and pull out the insides, trying to get as close to the sides and bottoms as you can without making any holes. (Don't throw

away the insides as they are fantastic for bread and butter pudding or posh breadcrumbs). Stuff them as full as you can with the filling, piling it a bit beyond the top. Scatter the remaining cheese on the stuffed brioches and put the lids back on.

4. Put the brioches on a baking sheet back in the pre-heated oven for about 20 minutes. They are ready when they are heated right through and the bits of filling which are showing are just beginning to colour.

White wine and tarragon sauce

25 g (1 oz) butter
½ medium red onion, very finely diced
1 small carrot, very finely diced
1 stick celery, very finely diced
1 generous tsp dried tarragon
350 ml (12 fl oz) white wine
Stock from the leek filling
350 ml (12 fl oz) whipping cream

1. In a pan melt the butter and sweat the finely diced onion, carrots and celery with a little salt and the dried tarragon until the vegetables are tender and giving off a little liquid. (If you are using fresh tarragon, add it at the same time as the cream – but beware, quite a lot of tarragon plants in gardens are the variety known as Russian tarragon which grows very vigorously but doesn't taste of very much.)

2. Add any leek stock left over from the filling and the white wine. Bring to the boil and boil fiercely, uncovered, for about 10 minutes to reduce the volume by about half.

3. Add the cream and bring back to the boil. Simmer until the sauce is the consistency of pouring cream. Take off the heat and season to taste with salt and pepper. This sauce will re-heat without any harm coming to it.

NEW SEASON CAULIFLOWER AND CARROTS IN TOMATO VINAIGRETTE

SERVES 6

1 good tomato (preferably plum, beef tomato will do)
1 tbsp balsamic vinegar (good balsamic is nice in this but not necessary)
1 tsp dark muscovado sugar
1 tbsp water
100 ml (4 fl oz) olive oil

1 medium cauliflower, in florets
500 g (1 lb) small new carrots with their green tops on
(the baby veg you get at supermarkets will not taste nearly as good as proper young carrots
from someone's garden; if buying from a supermarket the medium/small carrots labelled
'new season's' carrots are generally the best)

1. Make the dressing. Place the tomato, vinegar, sugar and water in a food processor and whizz to a purée. While still whizzing pour in the olive oil, to make an emulsion like a mayonnaise. Set aside.

2. Cut off the leaves of the carrots, leaving about 1 cm of green stalk attached to the carrot. Bring a large pan of water to the boil and cook first the carrots and then the cauliflower florets until not quite tender – this dish is half way between a salad and a hot vegetable, so the vegetables want to retain some firmness. As soon as the vegetables are cooked, drain, toss with the tomato vinaigrette and serve.

If you want to avoid the last minute rush of this method of preparation, cook the vegetables earlier, being sure to refresh and drain again as soon as they are cooked. Toss in the dressing and serve at room temperature.

GARLIC AND CHILLI
ROAST POTATOES

SERVES 6

1 kg (2 lb) large potatoes, cut in wedges with their skins on –
you will probably get between six and eight wedges per potato
4 tbsp sunflower oil
1 fresh chilli, finely chopped, with the seeds
2 cloves garlic, crushed
Salt

1. Pre-heat the oven to 230°C (450°F/Gas Mark 8).

2. In a large pan of boiling water, boil the potato wedges until cooked. The more cooked they are, the more fat and flavour they will absorb, but the more difficult they will become to handle and the more messy they will end up looking – the choice is yours.

3. Drain the potatoes and toss in the oil and some salt. Put on a roasting tin in the pre-heated oven for about 20 minutes, until they are just beginning to colour. Take out and turn gently in the garlic and chilli, adding a little more oil if necessary. Return to the oven and continue cooking until golden and crisp. (If you add the garlic and chilli at the beginning of the roasting process it tends to burn a little by the time the potatoes are ready.)

RHUBARB FOOL

SERVES 6

500 g (1 lb) rhubarb, in 2 cm (1 inch) lengths
40 g (1½ oz) light muscovado sugar
125 g (4 oz) Greek yoghurt
200 ml (7 fl oz) whipping cream

1. Wash and drain the rhubarb. Put with the sugar in a covered saucepan (aluminium is not good for cooking rhubarb), bring to the boil and simmer very gently with the lid on for about 5 minutes until the rhubarb is tender, but with any luck not too mushy. Take it off the heat, stir vigorously to break up the rhubarb, and leave to cool with the lid off. Once it has cooled a little, stir in the Greek yoghurt.

2. Half whip the cream. (In other words the cream should be at a sloppier stage than you want it to be by the time you have folded it in to the rhubarb mixture. If you whip it stiffly before folding it in, the folding process will cause it to split when you do fold it in.) Fold the cream in to the rhubarb mixture half at a time.

I think this is best served at a cool room temperature. It has a less luxurious texture once it has been refrigerated.

ALMOND BISCUITS

This recipe works better if you can start it the night before.

MAKES ABOUT 25 BISCUITS

125 g (4 oz) butter
200 g (7 oz) light muscovado sugar
1 egg
A few drops vanilla essence
125 g (4 oz) ground almonds
90 g (3 oz) plain flour
1 tsp baking powder
Pinch salt
25 g (1 oz) flaked almonds, toasted and chopped

The night before:

1. Cream the butter and sugar in a food processor.

2. Add the eggs and a few drops of vanilla essence and whizz again. Add the ground almonds, flour, baking powder and salt and whizz again.

3. Tip the mix into a big bowl and stir in the toasted flaked almonds. Cover with clingfilm and rest in the fridge overnight.

Next day:

1. Pre-heat the oven to 200°C (400°F/Gas Mark 6).

2. Line several large baking sheets with parchment.

3. Form the dough into balls the size of a walnut.

4. Place them well apart on the baking sheets and bake for 10–12 minutes.

5. Cool biscuits on a wire rack and store in an airtight container if you think they're likely to escape being eaten within the next few minutes.

Early spring supper

LUKE'S CORNISH CAULIFLOWER AND CORIANDER SOUP

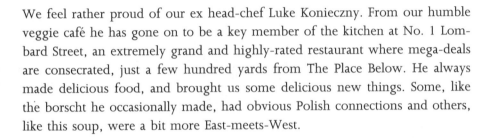

We feel rather proud of our ex head-chef Luke Konieczny. From our humble veggie café he has gone on to be a key member of the kitchen at No. 1 Lombard Street, an extremely grand and highly-rated restaurant where mega-deals are consecrated, just a few hundred yards from The Place Below. He always made delicious food, and brought us some delicious new things. Some, like the borscht he occasionally made, had obvious Polish connections and others, like this soup, were a bit more East-meets-West.

The West in this case means Cornwall, where the best cauliflowers in the UK come from. At this time of year you can pick up extraordinarily cheap, large, firm, creamy-coloured cauliflowers (confusingly referred to as broccoli by the locals) at roadside stalls throughout Cornwall. Cornish farmers apparently have great difficulty selling their crop to the supermarkets either because they are too large (?!) or because the curd is cream-coloured not white. Are we consumers really that stupid?

SERVES 4 WITH SOME LEFT OVER FOR THE NEXT DAY'S LUNCH

2 tbsp sunflower oil
2 cloves garlic, crushed
150 g (6 oz) onions, diced
1 dsp coriander seeds, roasted and ground
500 g (1 lb) potatoes, diced
1 smallish cauliflower, in florets
100 ml (3 fl oz) double cream
Salt, pepper and soy sauce

1. Sweat the onions and garlic in the oil until soft.

2. Add the freshly ground coriander seeds and cook for 2 more minutes.

3. Add the potatoes, cauliflower and water and simmer until the potatoes are soft.

4. Turn off the heat, add the cream and fresh coriander and blend thoroughly.

5. Season with salt, pepper and a very little soy sauce.

SPAGHETTI WITH QUICK PESTO, ROAST POTATOES AND SPRING CABBAGE

This is another recipe brought along to The Place Below by Luke. Like the recipe on page 253 (Post Xmas Pasta) this stars the unlikely combination of pasta and potatoes. If you think, as I did, that it sounds an odd idea, combining two starchy staples in the same dish, do not be put off. It is an exceptionally delicious combination with the sweet and crunchy young cabbage contrasting beautifully with the richly sauced pasta, and the tiny nuggets of roast potato.

At The Place Below we do this with fine beans, and occasionally asparagus, instead of the cabbage, but at home cabbage is my favourite – spring, primo or Savoy, anything except the nasty and pointless Dutch white. Note that if you use a slightly tougher sort of greens such as Cornish spring greens, you will need to put them in with the pasta earlier so that the pasta and the greens are cooked at the same moment.

In both restaurants, we use our Home-made Pesto (*see recipe on page xiii*), but if you don't have any already made up, this version saves getting out the blender (or indeed the pestle and mortar for any food Luddites out there). I haven't discovered any shop-bought bottled pesto which I like. It just doesn't taste nice, in this or any other dish.

1 largish potato (about 400 g/14 oz),
either washed or peeled, and diced very small, about the size of peas
3 tbsp olive oil
Salt and pepper

2 bunches of basil or 2 small supermarket-style basil plants
Juice of ½ a lemon
1 good clove garlic, crushed
150 ml (5 fl oz) olive oil
1 tsp salt
100 g (4 oz) freshly grated Parmesan

350 g (12 oz) spaghetti (dried)
½ a medium spring cabbage, about 400 g (14 oz), very finely shredded

1. Pre-heat the oven to 230°C (450°F/Gas Mark 8).

2. Turn the diced potatoes in 3 tbsp olive oil and season with salt and pepper. Spread on a baking sheet (on some baking parchment for ease of cleaning) and put in the oven for 20–30 minutes until golden. Turn them over when the bottoms are cooked.

3. Meanwhile make the pesto. Simply mix the basil, lemon juice, olive oil, garlic and salt together in a bowl, and then stir in the freshly grated Parmesan.

4. Bring a very large pan of salted water to the boil. Read your spaghetti packet to see how long the recommended cooking time is. Put the spaghetti into the boiling water, 3 minutes before the end of the cooking time add the cabbage and continue cooking. Test the spaghetti – there is no shortcut to taking a bit out and biting it – and when it is just done (but before it goes mushy) drain it. Don't worry about draining every drop, a tiny bit of cooking water clinging to the pasta and cabbage mixes nicely with the pesto.

5. Return the spaghetti and cabbage to the pan and mix thoroughly with the pesto and roast potato. Check the seasoning and serve at once.

Some other quick pasta ideas

If you want an ultra quick pasta sauce just gently warm (don't fry) some crushed garlic in plenty of olive oil and toss that with some spaghetti, salt, pepper and plenty of freshly grated parmesan – if you have 60 seconds longer add some grated lemon zest as well. If you have a further minute then chuck in some finely chopped parsley as well.

About this time of year, stir-fry some purple-sprouting broccoli in sunflower oil with ginger, garlic and chilli and then toss with macaroni.

Fry plenty of finely chopped leeks with a little dried tarragon; add some white wine and boil fiercely for 5 minutes, add double cream and bubble for another couple of minutes. Toss it all with just-cooked tagliatelle and a little crumbled Beenleigh Blue (*see page* 230) or Roquefort.

Boil some penne and 2 minutes before it is ready add some finely chopped cabbage. As soon as the pasta is cooked, drain the cabbage and pasta and toss with some truffle paste (a shop-bought puree of mushrooms blended with a little truffle), some olive oil and plenty of Parmesan.

In summer: De-seed a few plum tomatoes (halve them lengthways and scoop out the seeds as though they were little melons – it won't work so well with other kinds of tomatoes). Chop them finely and warm (on quite a low heat; you're not trying to cook the tomato pieces, just warm them) with some crushed garlic in plenty of olive oil. Toss with tagliatelle and a good handful of torn basil leaves. Serve with freshly grated Parmesan.

PASSION FRUIT SYLLABUB

Passion fruit appear to be virtually seasonless in their availability, but they are too delicious not to use. You want to look for fruit with a very wrinkled skin – smooth-skinned passion fruit are not ripe.

This was an idea I came across at Launceston Place Restaurant in London where I worked briefly in the 1980s. Exotic fruits were very much flavour of the month at that time, but passion fruit have a wonderful flavour and aroma which sets them above momentarily trendy but pointless fruit such as star-fruit.

This syllabub is lovely on its own, with ripe mango, and even with strawberries. It also makes the best possible filling for pavlova. If you want to make it even richer, use double cream instead of whipping.

SERVES 4 SWEET-TOOTHED PEOPLE OR 6 AVERAGE ONES

6 ripe passion fruit
3 tbsp caster sugar
300 ml (10 fl oz) whipping cream

1. Halve the passion fruit and scoop out the pulp. Put it in a blender with the sugar and whizz briefly. This is just to break up the flesh a little bit so that it mixes with the cream more easily.

2. Whip the cream until it is not quite stiff and then fold into the passion fruit purée. Serve either on plates or, more daintily, in glasses.

Seasonal pleasure: the cabbage family (brassicas)

This time of year, people often complain, is a low point in the vegetable calendar. Root vegetables are past their best and the spring and early summer treats of asparagus, new potatoes and strawberries have not yet arrived.

There are, however, plenty of brassicas – the cabbage family – around. I love almost all members of the cabbage family except, I have to admit, brussels sprouts. However briefly they are cooked they seem to have all the sulphurous nastiness of badly cooked cabbage, and none of the bitter-sweetness of properly treated brassicas.

Cabbage is generally delicious when cooked very briefly (e.g. rapidly boiled or stir-fried) or extremely slowly for a long time (e.g. red cabbage and apple or sauerkraut) but rather revolting when cooked for any period in between (e.g. school cabbage). There is a good scientific reason for the preference for brief cooking. Various smelly chemicals such as hydrogen sulphide (typical of rotting eggs) are produced when the cabbage tissue is broken down; while the cabbage is still growing they are bound to sugar molecules and are inactive. As the cabbage is cooked they are released and bind together to form even smellier compounds. For example, the amount of hydrogen sulphide produced in boiled cabbage doubles between the 5th and 7th minutes of cooking. For this and other much other fascinating information about the science of food, pulses and space-suits, see *On Food and Cooking* by Harold McGee (HarperCollins, 1984).

I have not found any scientific reason why very slow and long cooking should, by contrast, make cabbage very tasty, but it must be there somewhere, because it does.

Briefly cooked cauliflower and broccoli (ordinary or purple sprouting) make lovely winter salads. They should be dressed generously with either a Tomato Vinaigrette (*see page* 73) or citrus juice with olive oil. Chilli, garlic and ginger also go well with this family.

MAY

May is the month of the blessed marriage of
English asparagus and Jersey Royal New Potatoes.

May Day breakfast

Cider brandy and Dunkertons cocktail

Pink grapefruit with Alfonso mangoes

Scrambled eggs with morels and fried leftover new potatoes

Brioche with strawberry jam

English asparagus dinner

Asparagus and Jersey Royals tossed in tarragon butter

A gurgle of spring vegetables with a green pea,
mint and mascarpone blob

Crottin de Chavignol with onion marmalade

Alfonso mangoes – the world's finest variety of the
world's finest fruit – with lime juice

English asparagus supper

Asparagus, tarragon and parsley risotto

Frances' salad of avocado, Alfonso mango and baby gem lettuce
with a ginger and tahini dressing

Early strawberry and mascarpone cake

Seasonal pleasure: morels

Pasta with morels and baked garlic

May Day breakfast

Cider brandy and Dunkertons cocktail!
Pink grapefruit with Alfonso mangoes
Scrambled eggs with morels and fried leftover new potatoes
Brioche with strawberry jam

Just occasionally (or perhaps not so occasionally) the shout goes up for not only a large but also a special breakfast. It doesn't have to be on 1st May, but it's as good an excuse as any. These aren't things which require recipes, but are just ideas for enjoyment.

One of the great pleasures of coming to live in Hereford has been the easy availability of really excellent cider. And, for me, the best of all the Hereford ciders and perries are those made by Ivor and Susie Dunkerton. They have recently started producing a sparkling cider which is jam-packed with the taste of apples and has a beautiful balance of sweetness and acidity. We sell lots of it at Café @ All Saints, use it in a delicious prune and cider tart (see the recipe for prune and brandy tart in the first Place Below cookbook) and sometimes in bread and butter pudding. I also get through a frightening quantity of it at home. You can buy their cider easily in Hereford; most health food shops with a licence sell it (the Dunkertons are fiercely organic) and branches of Waitrose sell the sparkling cider. This cocktail was suggested to me by Ivor, and I think it's a fantastic and patriotic twist on a traditional champagne cocktail.

Put a sugar lump in the bottom of a champagne flute. Add a slug of cider brandy (now made in both Herefordshire and Somerset) or Calvados (if you are a good European) and fill to the top with a really good sparkling cider. Drink a glass and sink back in a gentle glow.

To penetrate this haze, make a refreshing fruit salad. Allow one pink grapefruit and one Alfonso mango (*see discussion on page 95*) for two people. Peel the grapefruit with a knife and segment it, leaving all the pith behind. Peel the mango and cut the flesh away from the stone, and cut into large chunks. Mix the two together with any juice left in the segmented grapefruit and serve.

This zesty fruit salad will have got your digestive juices ready for some more serious eating. Make sure that you boiled too many new potatoes the night before. Cut them in half lengthways and fry them in sunflower oil, turning regularly and seasoning towards the end of their cooking time.

Meanwhile, fry a few ounces of fresh morels if you can get them (one ounce of re-hydrated dried ones if you can't) in a generous knob of butter. After a couple of minutes add a splash of wine and a couple of tablespoons of double cream. Bubble away for a few minutes until the morels are tender and check the seasoning.

Finally, make a little scrambled egg – if you want instructions, see page 4. Divide eggs, potatoes and morels between plates and eat.

If you have space after that, warm some Home-made Brioches (see page 70) in the oven (unless of course you've made them that morning) and eat with the last of last year's home-made strawberry jam. Wash down with lots of fresh coffee.

English asparagus dinner

ASPARAGUS AND JERSEY ROYALS TOSSED IN TARRAGON BUTTER

This is just about the simplest way to enjoy the delicious and highly comple-
mentary flavours of Britain's finest new potatoes (or so Anton Mosimann
keeps telling us) and Britain's poshest vegetable. Actually, I'm going to come
clean here. I think Jersey Royals can be very good indeed. However, I have
found that, especially in the case of the earliest ones, they are not always as
earthy and flavoursome as other varieties, where perhaps there is less of a
contest to harvest them early for maximum prices. In fact, although it goes
against the philosophy of following local seasons, early Egyptian, Israeli and
Cyprus new potatoes can be very good indeed, as can other UK varieties such
as Maris Peer a little later in the season.

Last year I discovered a wonderful thing – picking your own asparagus. We
did this at Tillington Court Farm in Herefordshire. It is amazingly easy and sat-
isfying. We went back many times in the short season and I picked much of
Café @ All Saints' supply this way. Asparagus is one of those vegetables where
freshness makes all the difference. Being a city boy and not used to seeing vegetables growing in the ground, I found it utterly miraculous to see all these
beautiful green stems poking up out of the earth. Helpfully, at this particular
farm, you are forbidden to use a knife. This means that you snap the asparagus
stem at its natural breaking point, which is the method I would normally
adopt to trim the woody part off. In this way you waste not one millimetre of
what you pick. I'm already excited about going back there next year!

Another place to put on your mental asparagus map is the The Plough pub at
Ford in Gloucestershire. In season they have huge notices outside trumpeting
the availability of asparagus brought up from the Vale of Evesham just below,
and they serve asparagus with unmatched generosity, by the bundle or the

half bundle, with new potatoes, hollandaise, and various other accompaniments. It is also an extremely nice pub even if you miss the asparagus season.

If you want to be fractionally more elaborate serve hollandaise instead – either with lime juice as on page 68 or substituting lemon juice in the same recipe.

with lime juice as on page 68

SERVES 4–6 AS A STARTER

700 g (1½ lb) asparagus, trimmed of any woody part
1 kg (2 lb) new potatoes, e.g. Jersey Royals
150 g (5 oz) butter
1 bunch fresh tarragon, stripped from the stalks
Salt and pepper

1 lemon, cut into wedges, for a garnish

1. If you can be bothered, scrape the skins off the potatoes. This is not so much for the taste or texture, both of which I personally like, but because skinless potatoes seem to cook more evenly without falling apart. If you don't wish or can't be bothered to scrape them, just be careful about not over or under-cooking them.

2. Put the potatoes in a pan of cold water and bring to the boil. Simmer for about 15 minutes until they are cooked but not mushy and drain. Add a little butter and leave them to keep warm.

3. Meanwhile bring a large pan of water to the boil. Shortly before you are ready to eat put the trimmed asparagus in and bring back to the boil. I then boil it for only about 2 minutes, but some people prefer it more cooked than that, so taste as you go. When it is ready drain it thoroughly.

4. Meanwhile, gently heat the butter in a large frying pan and add the tarragon. Warm together over a low heat – you want to infuse the butter with the flavour of tarragon, not fry the herb. After a couple of minutes add the drained asparagus and potatoes and gently turn them in the tarragon butter. Season generously with salt and freshly ground black pepper and divide between warmed serving plates, making sure everyone gets their fair share of butter. Serve at once, perhaps garnished with a wedge of lemon.

A GURGLE OF SPRING VEGETABLES WITH A GREEN PEA, MINT AND MASCARPONE BLOB

This recipe is loosely based on something we ate at the most exciting French restaurant I have ever been to - Restaurant Michel Bras. It is an amazing place, a modern building like a spaceship perched on the top of bleak and beautiful moorland in the middle of the Massif Central. You eat looking out through a huge glass window over the hills, served by waiters in Armani-style pyjama suits who swish in and out through electric doors like officers on the Starship Enterprise. The chef-patron, Michel Bras, is a rare French cook with a passion for vegetables, herbs and mushrooms.

A dish for which he is well known is his 'Gargouillou', a beautifully composed selection of vegetables cooked in a vegetable stock. This is my version of this idea – I'm not sure if gurgle is the correct translation but I rather like the idea of a 'gurgle' of vegetables. It is a slightly fiddly recipe but tastes and looks delicious – even more so if you are lucky enough to have any of the vegetables fresh from your own garden. It must be eaten as soon as it is ready and is delicious both on its own or served with a bit of the green pea, mint and mascarpone blob on each portion.

The deliciousness does depend on getting hold of lovely vegetables. In particular, if you can find decent-sized new season carrots – normally sold in bunches with their tops still on – they are a big improvement over either huge very old carrots, or pointless baby carrots the size of your little finger.

SERVES 6

2 large bulbs garlic (30–40 cloves)
1.2 litres (2 pints) water
125 ml (4 fl oz) white wine
2 large leeks, sliced
1 bulb fennel, roughly chopped

250 g (9 oz) spinach, washed and roughly chopped
25 g (1 oz) sorrel, washed and roughly chopped

200 g (7 oz) new season carrots, sliced diagonally,
retaining about 1 cm of the carrot tops if you have them
125 g (5 oz) very fine asparagus (also sold as 'sprue asparagus')
200 g (7 oz) broccoli (or purple sprouting if available), in florets
125 g (5 oz) courgettes, in batons
200 g (7 oz) sugar snap peas, topped and tailed

1. Break the garlic into cloves but do not peel. Bring a pan of water to the boil. Put the unpeeled garlic into the water, bring it back to the boil, simmer for one minute and then drain, discarding the water. Put the garlic into cold water for a couple of minutes and then drain again. The garlic should be very easy to peel at this point. Peel it and put back in the pan with 1.2 litres (2 pints) of water and the wine. Bring to the boil and simmer for about 20 minutes. Add the chopped leeks and fennel and continue to simmer for a further 20 minutes. Drain the stock through a fine sieve, pushing some of the cooked garlic and vegetables through the sieve. Discard the remainder of the garlic and the vegetables.

2. Place the washed but still wet spinach and sorrel in a large covered pan and cook on a medium heat for about 7 minutes until the spinach is quite wilted. Take the spinach and sorrel out of the pan and set aside.

3. When everyone is ready to eat, start the final stage. Make sure you have some soup dishes warming. Put the stock in a large pan and bring it to the boil. Add the carrots and asparagus and bring it back to the boil. Simmer for 2 minutes and then add the broccoli, courgettes and sugar snap peas. Bring back to the boil and simmer for a further 2 minutes. Meanwhile divide the spinach and sorrel between the soup plates. As soon as the other vegetables are ready, take them off the heat and arrange them in elegant piles on top of the little heaps of spinach and sorrel. Divide the stock between the plates, top each dish with an elegant blob (otherwise known as a quenelle) of green pea, mint and mascarpone and serve at once – offer knife, fork and spoon to eat with.

Green pea, mint and mascarpone blob

Many of the delicious things we serve at The Place Below have come to the restaurant via Ian Burleigh, the manager. This blob (or dip or quenelle as it might be called by the more genteel among us) is based on something he used to serve in his former restaurant, Bart's, in Ashtead, Surrey.

If you are a pea grower, you will think that this recipe comes a few weeks early. However, it is excellent made with frozen peas – and your garden mint should certainly be flourishing by now.

As well as being delicious with the Gurgle of Vegetables described above, it makes a great dip for crudités or tortilla chips.

SERVES 6

250 g (8 oz) green peas, shelled weight (fresh or frozen)
6 good sprigs of mint, the leaves stripped from the stalks
250 g (8 oz) mascarpone

1. Bring a pan of water to the boil. Add the peas and mint leaves. Bring back to the boil and drain. Put in a blender with the mascarpone. Whizz until it has made a very smooth puree. Chill until you need it.

CROTTIN DE CHAVIGNOL
WITH ONION MARMALADE

Crottins de Chavignol are exceptionally delicious individual little goat's cheeses which I believe charmingly translate as 'small turds from Chavignol'. It's that rural way with picturesque language. If you can't get hold of them then circles cut off any decent mature goat's cheese log would be OK. If you are within striking distance of West London, make these goat's cheeses an excuse to visit Vivian's in Richmond, a fantastic salivating Aladdin's cave of cheeses, oils, coffees and other excellent things. When you are exhausted with tasting and shopping there, have lunch at the White Horse pub just behind, one of the happy new generation of pubs which have been transformed from tired fruit machine boozer, to serious but good value food establishment, which nevertheless still sells decent beer.

The onion marmalade will make about double what you want for this, but it keeps well in the fridge and is delicious in cheese sandwiches or with toasted cheese.

SERVES 6

3 tbsp olive oil
750 g (1½ lb) onions, halved and finely sliced
2 tbsp balsamic vinegar
1 tbsp molasses sugar
Salt and pepper

100 g (4 oz) rocket leaves
1 tbsp walnut oil

6 Crottins de Chavignol, or 1 small mature goat's cheese log
cut into 6 generous slices

1. In a heavy-bottomed pan, heat the oil. Add the onions and fry over a high heat for about 20 minutes, stirring every 2–3 minutes so that the onions brown in between stirrings, but do not burn.

2. Add the vinegar, sugar and salt and cook fiercely for a minute. Take off the heat. Taste and adjust the salt, sugar and vinegar. This will keep well in the fridge for a few days, but be sure to allow it to come up to room temperature before serving.

3. Pre-heat the grill.

4. When you are just about ready to eat, toss the rocket leaves in the walnut oil and some salt and pepper and divide between plates and put a dollop of onion marmalade on the the side of each plate. Put the goat's cheeses under the grill for a couple of minutes until they are just beginning to melt and put on top of the pile of salad leaves. Serve at once.

ALFONSO MANGOES – THE WORLD'S FINEST VARIETY OF THE WORLD'S FINEST FRUIT – WITH LIME JUICE

This is not a recipe, but it is one of the most delicious eating experiences available in the world. The Alfonso is a variety of mango grown in India. They vary in size but are generally not as large as the mangoes you see in the supermarkets. They are distinguished by an intense perfume, and a lack of fibre. Following the Alfonso season there are similar varieties flown in from Pakistan, so the season for this style of mango extends from April until August.

I have never seen them for sale in supermarkets, and your best bet is to find them in street markets in Asian areas of big cities. Southall is overflowing with Alfonsoes – sold by the box not by the mango – in season. So make this an excuse to have a day of excellent curry and lassi eating and pick up a couple of cases of mangoes for gorging yourself (and possibly friends and family) over the next few days.

You can do elaborate things with them. (They go beautifully with Passion Fruit Syllabub (*see page 82*) or in a fruit salad with pink grapefruit (*see page 86*) or in a Salad with a Creamy Tahini Dressing (*see page 98*) but best of all, peel them, cut the flesh away from the stone and squeeze a little lime juice over it. Allow at least one mango per person and don't chop them up long before you want to eat them. A little lime juice is also the best accompaniment for really ripe papaya.

English asparagus supper

ASPARAGUS, TARRAGON
AND PARSLEY RISOTTO

This is a pretty, creamy and elegant supper dish. Asparagus and tarragon go beautifully together.

One good bunch of asparagus should leave you with a bit left over after using the stalks for the risotto base and the tops to spread on top. This is one of the few recipes in this book where you really do need to use a stock (as opposed to just water) to cook with. If you aren't in the habit of making your own, Marigold is an excellent brand of vegetable stock powder.

SERVES 2

4 tbsp olive oil
100 g (4 oz) leeks, small dice
1 small stick celery, small dice
75 g (3 oz) asparagus stalks, chopped
1 tsp dried tarragon

250 ml (9 fl oz) dry white wine
450 ml (16 fl oz) vegetable stock, either home-made or made with Marigold bouillon powder

150 g (5½ oz) risotto rice
200 g (7 oz) long asparagus tops
1 tbsp olive oil
Salt and freshly ground black pepper

75 g (3 oz) fresh grated Parmesan
1 really large bunch of parsley (either flat-leaf or curly – I prefer flat-leaf), very finely chopped
25 g (1 oz) butter

1. Put the leeks, celery, asparagus bottoms and dried tarragon in a heavy-bottomed pan over a medium heat. Add a little salt and stir regularly for about 10 minutes until the vegetables are soft.

2. Meanwhile put the wine and stock to heat in a separate pan. Turn this off just before it boils.

3. At the same time in a third pan heat some water for blanching the asparagus tops.

4. When the onion/celery mixture is soft, add the rice and asparagus bottoms. Immediately add a ladleful of the wine/stock mixture. Turn up high until it starts bubbling and then turn down and keep cooking, stirring constantly. When most of the liquid has been absorbed add some more of the wine/stock and continue cooking as before. Continue doing this until you have used most of the wine/stock. Then check to see if the rice is cooked. There should still be some resistance in the grain but it should have lost its raw, woody texture. The risotto should at this stage be the consistency of a sloppy stew or a very thick soup. If the rice is not quite cooked add the rest of the wine/stock and continue cooking for another couple of minutes. Check that the rice is now cooked. If it is still not cooked add a little boiling water and continue cooking. The whole process will take about 20 minutes, depending on how hard you boil the risotto.

5. Meanwhile, when the risotto looks nearly ready, put the asparagus tops in the boiling water. Bring back to the boil and boil for about 2 minutes until they are just tender. Drain well, put back in the pan and toss in the seasoned olive oil. Leave on one side while you finish off the risotto.

6. Once the rice is cooked, take off the heat, stir in the parsley, butter and Parmesan and check the seasoning.

Serve at once, topping each plate of risotto with its asparagus tops.

FRANCES' SALAD OF AVOCADO, ALFONSO MANGO AND BABY GEM LETTUCE WITH A GINGER AND TAHINI DRESSING

The sweet tahini dressing makes a lovely partner for mango and avocado in this very simple salad.

The salad quantities are for two people but you will have plenty of dressing left over.

SERVES 2

½ a knob of stem ginger
½ tbsp French mustard (smooth not grainy)
1 tbsp runny honey
Juice of 1 lemon
2 tbsp tahini
4 tbsp water
½ tsp salt
4 tbsp olive oil

1 baby gem lettuce, the leaves separated and washed
1 smallish mango (preferably Alfonso)
1 small ripe avocado

1. Make the dressing. Put all the dressing ingredients except the olive oil in a blender and whizz until smooth. Add the olive oil and whizz again until the oil has emulsified (i.e. you can't see separate bits of oil). Adjust the seasoning to taste.

2. Arrange the lettuce leaves on two plates. Peel the mango. Slice the flesh off the stone – work parallel to the flat side of the stone. Arrange the mango slices on the lettuce. Shortly before you are ready to eat, halve the avocado, take the stone out and peel the two halves. Cut each half into about three fat strips and arrange on top of the salad. Dribble a couple of tablespoons of dressing over each plate and leave the jug on the table for more if wanted.

EARLY STRAWBERRY AND MASCARPONE CAKE

We mostly make this dish with raspberries but it is also lovely with really flavoursome strawberries – a kind of trifle made into a cake. In most of its guises I'm not over-excited by mascarpone (Italian cream cheese) but this cake has enough booze and fruit in it to counter the somewhat cloying effect of the cheese.

150 ml (5 fl oz) milk
90 ml (3 fl oz) single cream

25 g (1 oz) cornflour
1 egg yolk
1 egg
90 g (3 oz) icing sugar
1 tsp vanilla essence
450 g (1 lb) mascarpone

1 packet of sponge fingers (you'll probably have some left over for dunking in your tea)
300 ml (10 fl oz) Marsala
375 g (13 oz) strawberries, hulled and quartered

200 g (7 oz) amaretti biscuits, crushed roughly (not to a powder)
A little cocoa powder

19 cm (7½ inch) springform cake tin, lined

1. Heat the milk and cream to boiling point. Mix the cornflour, egg yolk and eggs, icing sugar and vanilla essence together and pour onto the hot milk/cream mixture. Pour back into the saucepan and heat gently, stirring constantly, until the custard begins to thicken. Tip out of the pan straight away and allow to cool. When it is cool, mix with the mascarpone.

2. In the lined tin, layer the cake as follows: Sponge fingers, Marsala, custard, strawberries, sponge fingers, Marsala, strawberries, custard. Leave to chill in the fridge overnight (any shorter and it will probably fall apart).

3. The next day, turn out the cake. Press the biscuits into the sides and top. Dust the top with cocoa powder. Serve.

Seasonal pleasure: morels

Morels are the weirdest looking and most delicious of wild mushrooms – their honeycomb structure looks like the brain of some creature from a science fiction story. Together with the tiny mousserons (which I think are rather less interesting) they are the only edible wild mushrooms available from this end of Europe at this time of year. The wild mushroom trade is now going the way of all other products and you can find almost any kind of mushroom at any time of year, if you are prepared to pay for them, sourced from America, Africa, Europe and China as the season moves around the globe. But for really fresh wild mushrooms at a remotely sensible price, stick to the European seasons.

Having said that, morels are almost never to be found at a very sensible price. They are rarely found in the UK, preferring warmer, drier climates (France and Italy), and unless you live within reach of Tony Booth's shop (*see page* 3), or a handful of others in the country which are serious about fresh wild mushrooms, you will have to make do with dried morels.

I only mention them at all because they are so delicious and beautiful. If the cepe is the prince of mushrooms the morel is the king. Like most genuinely wild things – as opposed, for instance, to shitake and oyster mushrooms, which are almost invariably cultivated – they come in widely varying sizes, from the size of a broad bean to the size of a mouse. As well as their strong flavour, their other great quality is that, unlike most other mushrooms, they keep their shape and do not give off a lot of juice. This means that their cooking medium has to be fairly wet or you have to use a fairly generous quantity of butter or oil to fry them in.

They make a delicious canapé when stuffed with a mushroom and cream cheese purée or on a kebab with baby preserved onions (cipollini – available in Italian delicatessens); and they are wonderful in all kinds of rich mushroom sauces such as this one to be served with pasta.

PASTA WITH MORELS
AND BAKED GARLIC

3 heads garlic (preferably new season garlic with green tops,
available only at this time of year), the cloves separated but not peeled
25 g (1 oz) butter
2 tbsp olive oil
200 g (7 oz) fresh morels — any size, if they are large, chop them in two
1 big sprig of fresh thyme (don't substitute dried thyme)
300 ml (10 fl oz) red wine
200 ml (7 fl oz) double cream
250 g (8 oz) pasta e.g. penne
Parmesan to grate at table

1. Pre-heat oven to 230°C (450°F/Gas Mark 8).

2. Put the garlic in a pan of boiling water for one minute, then drain and refresh in cold water and drain again. Peel the garlic and bake in the pre-heated oven for about 10 minutes until tender and smelling nutty.

3. In a pan, heat the butter and oil. Add the morels and fry for a couple of minutes. Add the sprig of thyme and wine and reduce to half its volume on a high heat. Add the baked garlic and cream, bring back to the boil and simmer for a couple of minutes. Check the seasoning, remembering that the sauce is going with a fairly large quantity of pasta and should be strongly seasoned. Remove the sprig of thyme.

4. Meanwhile, cook the pasta. Bring plenty of salted water to boil in a large pan. Add the pasta and bring back to a rolling boil, cooking for a minute or so less than the time recommended on the packet. Test the pasta and if it is ready (if not ready leave a minute longer and try again) drain it and mix with the morel and garlic sauce. Serve at once on warmed plates with Parmesan to grate at the table if people want it.

JUNE

Early summer six course celebration dinner

Globe artichoke hollandaise

Carrot mousse with samphire and young carrots vinaigrette

Tiny pizza with beetroot, potatoes and fresh goat's cheese

Asparagus in nori with dill dressing

Strawberries in a balsamic syrup

Spiced gooseberry crème brûlée

Seasonal pleasures: eating peas and broad beans out of the pod

Early summer vegetables with fresh herbs, olive oil, lemon and Caerphilly

Summer garden pasta

Whole strawberry jam

Early summer six course celebration dinner

GLOBE ARTICHOKE HOLLANDAISE

Globe artichokes rate alongside morels and asparagus as one of the most sensuously beautiful things to eat. The process of eating them is also full of pleasure. Buttery fingers, communal dumping plates, a small amount of deliciously flavoured vegetables with plenty of sauce. They are not something I would want to eat every day, but for a feast, they are perfect.

For the hollandaise recipe, see page 68.

Allow one medium-sized artichoke per person.

Bring a very large pan of acidulated water to the boil (2 tbsp white wine vinegar to every litre of water). The vinegar in the water is to prevent the artichokes turning black. If they do turn black in parts this does not affect the flavour but they don't look so pretty. Cut the artichokes off just below the base and put them into the boiling water stem side down. If you have a lid slightly smaller than the size of pan you are using, that will help to keep the artichokes below the surface of the water, and therefore stay green, while they are cooking. Bring the water back to the boil and simmer for about 30 minutes.

To check if they are ready, take a leaf from the base of the largest artichoke and pull. If they are ready it should come off easily and the flesh at the base of the leaf should be tender but not mushy. If they are not ready, keep cooking, testing every 10 minutes or so. When they are ready, drain thoroughly. If you want to serve them hot, but nevertheless cook them ahead of time, they heat up very well in the microwave, or you can re-boil them briefly.

To make the eating easier for lazy guests – or those who are worried by the mildly complicated process of eating an artichoke – you can take out the chokes in advance. After the artichokes have been cooked and cooled just enough to handle, pull out the small central leaves in one bunch. You should then have exposed the choke, that is the grassy fibres which poke up from the artichoke heart. Taking a sharp dessertspoon, and working from the edge, scrape underneath the choke, trying to remove it as far as possible all in one piece. Make sure you have got rid of all the prickly grassy bits by further scraping with a spoon. This is a slightly tricky operation, which is only worth doing if you enjoy fiddling about with vegetables. Having done it you can then fill the hollow with hollandaise, and put an extra blob on the side. This looks very pretty, makes the artichokes easier to eat, but is a bit of a faff.

CARROT MOUSSE WITH SAMPHIRE AND YOUNG CARROTS VINAIGRETTE

Samphire, also known as 'sea asparagus', is most commonly seen in fish shops and fish restaurants. It is, however, a delicious vegetable, which deserves to be more widely used. It grows near the sea on rocks and cliffs. Most of the British crop apparently comes from Norfolk, where (so a regular customer at The Place Below tells me) children are paid miserably small sums for bringing it to market. Samphire for the restaurant trade tends to come from Brittany, where it is cleaned, sorted and presented much more beautifully than its British counterpart and costs four times as much.

Outside the summer season, you can (occasionally) buy pickled samphire, which has neither the colour nor the flavour of the fresh vegetable – don't bother.

It is lovely served hot with hollandaise, cold (as here) with a vinaigrette, and also in potato cakes with a sorrel and white wine sauce. To prepare it, wash it thoroughly and cut off any hard knobbly bits. Restaurants tend to trim it to an excessive extent; home eaters are perfectly able to discard any tough bits which end up on their plates. Some cookbooks tell you to blanch the samphire twice before boiling it to make it less salty, but I think this is a bad idea since part of its attraction is its saltiness.

The carrots to look for are what supermarkets have started calling 'new season carrots' (although, curiously, these new season carrots are for sale even in December), with the tops on and between the size of a large carrot and a baby carrot. For the salad part of the recipe, trim the top to a centimetre away from the carrot and then cut the whole thing in half lengthways. If you are a gardener, then of course your own carrots will be infinitely preferable.

This is both a very pretty and a delicious plateful.

SERVES 6

50 g (2 oz) butter
500 g (1 lb) carrots, sliced thickly
200 ml (4 fl oz) full fat Greek yoghurt
100 ml (4 fl oz) single cream
4 eggs
150 g (5 oz) finely grated Parmesan

250 g (8 oz) samphire
250 g (8 oz) new season's carrots with their tops on
250 g (8 oz) fresh peas (podded weight), for garnish

Olive oil
Juice of ½ a lemon
A few mint leaves, finely chopped
Salt and pepper

1. Preheat oven to 180°C (350°F/Gas Mark 4).

2. In a heavy-bottomed pan sweat the sliced carrots in the butter with some salt for about 20 minutes until they are very soft. Put in a food processor with the yoghurt, cream, eggs and Parmesan. Blend thoroughly and check the seasoning.

3. Grease six medium sized ramekins and divide the purée evenly between them. Put in a deep baking tray and half fill it with water to create a bain-marie. Put in the oven for about 45 minutes until the mousse is set. Allow to cool, ease away from the edge of the ramekin with a sharp knife, and turn the mousses out onto the serving plates.

4. Meanwhile, bring a large pan of water to the boil. Add the new season's carrots and bring back to the boil. Simmer until partly cooked (about 3 minutes); add the samphire and bring back to the boil. After another minute add the peas. As soon as the water has come back to the boil, drain it all and toss immediately in the olive oil, lemon juice and mint and season with salt and pepper. Put a little pile of this warm salad by each mousse – or, for greater elegance, make a circle around each plate with the mousse in the middle.

TINY PIZZA WITH BEETROOT, POTATOES AND FRESH GOAT'S CHEESE

As I pointed out in the first Place Below cookery book, pizzas started off as a way of using up leftover bread dough, and I often make a pizza with a bit of leftover bread dough (of whatever sort) and leftovers from the fridge. However, if I am making a pizza from scratch, this is the dough that I use. For the best results, you want a very simple, fairly slack dough, without any oil in it – there will be plenty of richness in the topping. According to the Neapolitan Pizza Association, you also need an oven at 800°F (if I remember the figure correctly). This is impossible in any normal oven, whether domestic or commercial, but you can get excellent results by turning your oven up to 475°F, or as high as it will go. Fussing around with pizza stones (a stone which you pre-heat in the oven before slipping the pizza on to it) I think is unnecessary.

Many cheeses work better on pizzas if they are added part way through the cooking process. If you ever make a pizza with Parmesan shavings on top (which can be delicious), they shouldn't have more than a minute in the oven.

Note that for best results you should have baked the beetroot before starting this recipe (*see page 198 for details*).

You need a fresh goat's cheese with a curdy texture for this pizza. In both London and Hereford we use the delicious Perroche log from Neal's Yard Creamery (also fantastic in a salad with roast sweet potatoes) which I was excited to discover is about six miles outside Hereford in an idyllic spot on a hill between the Golden Valley and Wye Valley.

Pizza dough

550 g (1 lb 4 oz) strong white flour
10 g (½ oz) salt
1 sachet easy blend yeast
400 ml (14 fl oz) water

Pizza topping and garnish

150 ml (5 fl oz) olive oil
750 g (1½ lb) onions, halved and sliced
2 cloves garlic, crushed
2 tbsp cheap balsamic vinegar
1 tbsp sugar

200 g (7 oz) new potatoes, skins scraped off or not as you prefer
250 g (8 oz) beetroot, baked the day before (see page 198)

200 g (7 oz) mild fresh goat's cheese (e.g. Neal's Yard Perroche log), crumbled
1 bunch chives, finely snipped
125 g (4 oz) rocket
Salt and pepper

1. Make the dough. Mix all the ingredients together and knead for 10 minutes. Leave in the mixing bowl covered with clingfilm, or a damp cloth, until doubled in size.

2. Oil a large baking sheet. Divide the dough into six, and roll out into thin discs about six inches in diameter, put on the baking sheet and leave in a warm place. The bases need to prove for at least 20 minutes in a warm place, but can happily be left for much longer if that is convenient.

3. Fry the onions in the olive oil. After about 5 minutes add the garlic and continue cooking on a moderate heat for about 20 minutes until the onions are very soft. Add the vinegar, sugar and some salt and pepper and bubble fiercely for a couple of minutes, then turn off the heat.

4. Boil the new potatoes until just cooked and slice thickly. Peel the beetroot and slice thickly. Turn the beetroot and potatoes in the onion mixture and check the seasoning. Divide the mixture between the pizza bases and spread out evenly.

5. Pre-heat the oven to 230°C (450°F/Gas Mark 8). Bake the pizzas for 10 minutes as they are. Take them out and top with the crumbled goat's cheese and bake for a further 10 minutes. Take out, garnish with snipped chives and rocket leaves and serve. (The cooking times may be reduced somewhat if you can get your oven hotter than this.)

ASPARAGUS IN NORI
WITH DILL DRESSING

This might sound rather exotic but it's quite simple to make, and I think the taste of seaweed and dill go well with asparagus. It also looks extremely pretty. If you haven't used nori seaweed before, see the discussion on page 172. As always when serving seaweed (or tofu), I would recommend not telling people what they are eating until after they've eaten some of it!

The quantities are quite small as this is designed to be part of a many-coursed meal – double the quantities of asparagus and nori for a more generous sized starter. If there is any dill dressing left over have it with globe artichokes or salad potatoes. Dried dill is no use for this recipe (or for any other recipe).

SERVES 6

500 g (1 lb) asparagus, trimmed of any woody bits

1 tbsp soy sauce
1 tsp English mustard
6 sheets sushi nori

1 bunch dill
1 tsp Dijon mustard
1 tsp lemon juice
1 good tsp runny honey
2 tbsp olive oil

1. Bring a large pan of water to the boil. Put the asparagus in and bring back to the boil. Simmer for a couple of minutes. Take out one piece to see if it is cooked. If not, continue simmering for another minute and repeat.

2. As soon as the asparagus is tender, drain and plunge into cold water to stop it cooking any further. Drain again, very thoroughly this time.

3. Make a thin paste out of the soy sauce and English mustard. Brush this sparingly onto one sheet of nori. Divide the asparagus into six bundles and put the first bundle onto the first sheet of nori with the tops of the asparagus poking over the edge of the bottom right hand corner. Fold the left hand side of the sheet over the stalks and then roll the asparagus up. You should be left with a cigar with asparagus ends poking out. Repeat with the other five bundles.

4. Mix all the remaining ingredients together except the olive oil, then gradually add the olive oil, whisking as you go to emulsify the dressing.

5. Give everyone one asparagus bundle with a generous dribble of dressing over it.

STRAWBERRIES IN BALSAMIC SYRUP

When I first heard of the idea serving strawberries with balsamic vinegar I thought it sounded disgusting, but I'm now completely persuaded. You do need to use a good quality balsamic vinegar. At home I use a delicious vinegar from the Fresh Olive Company which has the viscosity of cough mixture and an intense sweet and sour flavour – I can eat it by the spoonful. It is not cheap, however.

For six people take 750 g (1½ lb) halved and hulled strawberries. To start with, add 2 teaspoons of balsamic vinegar and 2 tablespoons of caster sugar. Gently turn the strawberries in the sugar and vinegar. Leave to marinade for half an hour or so at room temperature. Adjust vinegar and sugar to taste. Stir gently but thoroughly before serving. If you are using an ordinary supermarket balsamic vinegar you may want to start with just 1 teaspoonful. The idea is not that the strawberries should taste of vinegar, but that there is a background sweet and sour taste which strengthens their flavour. Incidentally, Passion Fruit Syllabub (*see page 82*) makes a wonderful and luxurious partner for strawberries done in this way.

The same method works well for fresh ripe figs. Cut the figs into quarters and proceed as for the strawberries.

SPICED GOOSEBERRY CRÈME BRÛLÉE

The combination of sharp gooseberries, cream and fragrant spices is rather mediaeval, and really delicious.

I've been nervous of making crème brûlée for a long time. I think that the thing is on the one hand to be brave cooking the custard and not take it off the heat too soon; but also not to make it when you are in a hurry. Nearly all cookbooks instruct you to keep cooking the custard until it coats the back of a wooden spoon. This seems to me unhelpful since it will coat the back of the spoon to some extent the minute you put it into the pan, but if you take it off the heat straight away you will end up with completely liquid cream. I think that the only solution is to do it a few times, being sure to take it too far (at which point you get bits of cooked egg floating in the custard) a few times so that you get a feel for how the custard changes as it cooks. If it does scramble a little you can whizz it in a food processor or with a hand-held blender and you will have a perfectly acceptable custard, if not quite as silky smooth as it would have been if it had been taken off the heat at just the right moment.

I think that the topping is most delicious made with a good dark brown sugar such as a dark muscovado or molasses sugar. This has the advantage that if some of the sugar doesn't get grilled properly it still tastes delicious.

175 g (6 oz) gooseberries
40 g (1½ oz) caster sugar

400 ml (14 fl oz) double cream
1 cinnamon stick
3 cardamom pods, bruised
½ vanilla pod or ½ tsp vanilla essence
1 star anise
Peel of 1 lemon

4 egg yolks

Dark brown sugar

1. Put the gooseberries and sugar in a small pan and cook on a low heat with the lid on until the gooseberries are tender. Remove the gooseberries with a slotted spoon, divide between six small ramekins and put these in the fridge (or deep freeze if you have room) while you get on with the rest of the recipe.

2. If there is more than a drop of syrup in the bottom, bring it to the boil and boil fiercely for a couple of minutes to reduce to a sticky syrup.

3. Add the cream, spices and lemon peel to the gooseberry syrup. Bring to the boil and simmer gently for 10 minutes then take off the heat.

4. Put the egg yolks in a medium-sized heavy-bottomed pan and strain the cream into them, whisking as you go.

5. Put the pan over a fairly low heat and stir constantly for 5–10 minutes until the custard thickens. Take it off the heat and briefly whisk it once more to distribute the more cooked bits. Pour into the chilled ramekins and return to the fridge to chill thoroughly for at least 4 hours, preferably overnight.

6. Pre-heat the grill as hot as possible. Sprinkle a teaspoon of sugar evenly over each custard. If you have a spray gun, give the sugar a quick spray of water as this helps it to caramelise. Put the ramekins under the very hot grill until the sugar caramelises, checking every 30 seconds or so. This should only take a couple of minutes. If you smell burning take them out straight away.

7. Return to the fridge for half an hour or so before serving. You should have a crunchy top, a fragrant creamy custard, and palate freshening gooseberries buried at the bottom.

(See also page 185 for an ultra simplified version of crème brûlée made with grapes and sour cream.)

Seasonal pleasures: eating peas and broad beans out of the pod

I am a latecomer to the business of growing your own vegetables and in my first year I've had very mixed results. However, I'm finding it a really exciting business, and I'm already planning my next year's planting.

Fresh peas and beans are really quite different from the frozen variety, but only if they are very fresh indeed. In fact, I think that frozen peas can be quite good (broad beans less so) and are much better than peas in the pod which were picked too old or several days previously. So the best way to eat really fresh peas and broad beans is as you pick them, straight out of the pod. Young broad beans eaten this way are not even remotely floury, and tiny peas are just delicious.

One of the most memorable tastes from my first year's vegetable growing was harvesting my first little Charlotte potatoes (in late June), boiling them and tossing them with seasoned crème fraîche and freshly-picked and podded raw peas. Sarah and I ate plate after plate of this simple dish, and I'm convinced that's why we've ended up with a fat and healthy baby.

The whole process of podding peas and beans is a fairly time-consuming, but I think most pleasurable, activity. I still gasp with excitement at the soft bedding of a broad-bean pod, and the delicate pretty shape of a thin-skinned pea shell.

EARLY SUMMER VEGETABLES WITH FRESH HERBS, OLIVE OIL, LEMON AND CAERPHILLY

This recipe is only slightly more elaborate than eating peas and beans straight from the pod and like most of the simplest recipes, it relies heavily on the quality of the ingredients. You must use new potatoes (not simply the small main crop potatoes known in the trade as 'mids'), and there is no point making it unless you can get hold of really flavoursome young carrots (again, not the tiny baby carrots sold in supermarkets which are small but not generally flavoursome) and very fresh peas and beans.

It makes a really delicious supper or lunch, and (so long as you get help with podding the peas and beans) is very quick to prepare.

750 g (1½ lb) potatoes, scrubbed but not peeled
Mint, about five small sprigs
10–15 large leaves of sorrel, finely chopped
100 ml (3½ fl oz) olive oil
Juice of half a lemon

500 g (1 lb) young carrots with their tops on, cut thickly and diagonally
300 g (10 oz) fresh broad beans (podded weight)
250 g (8 oz) fresh peas (podded weight)

200 g (7 oz) good Caerphilly (e.g. Duckett's or Gorwyd), in small cubes

1. Boil the potatoes until just cooked with a couple of the sprigs of mint.

2. While the potatoes are cooking, bring a second pan of water to the boil.

3. Meanwhile, chop the remainder of the mint finely and mix with the finely chopped sorrel and the olive oil and lemon juice in a very large bowl.

4. Drain the potatoes and cut in half (quarters if they are large new potatoes) and mix while still very hot with the oil and herbs.

5. Put the carrots in the second pan of boiling water, bring back to the boil and boil for just 2–3 minutes until they are no longer crunchy but still quite firm. Remove from the pan with a slotted spoon or 'spider' and mix with the potatoes. Repeat the process with the peas and beans, which need cooking for only a minute or so (perhaps closer to a couple of minutes for the beans) – check whether they are done by tasting. Add to the mixing bowl and season generously with salt and freshly ground pepper.

6. Add half the cubed cheese and mix again. Use the remainder of the cheese to garnish individual plates. That way you get half the cheese melted in with the hot vegetables, and half in little salty bursts on top.

7. Ideally this dish is served very warm but not piping hot – a sort of 'salade super-tiede' as it might have been called in 1980. Surprisingly, it also heats up quite well the next day.

SUMMER GARDEN PASTA

Forget bottles of pesto. This is the authentic taste of fresh herbs, summer vegetables and extra virgin olive oil. Totally simple and utterly delicious. It is also
infinitely variable. Use the best vegetables to hand. Although the ingredients
of this are similar to those in the previous recipe, they're put together in a
different way and both are really worth trying.

SERVES 4

350 g (12 oz) new potatoes (e.g. Charlottes), diced the size of peas
100 ml (4 fl oz) olive oil
1 clove garlic, crushed
Good handful of chopped mint
Salt and freshly ground black pepper

500 g (1 lb) pasta, e.g. farfalle
300 g (10 oz) broccoli, in florets with the tender parts of the stems cut thinly and diagonally
150 g (5 oz) broad beans (podded weight)
200 g (7 oz) peas (podded weight)

150 g (5 oz) fresh grated Parmesan

1. Boil the diced potatoes for about 10 minutes until just cooked. Drain and
   toss with the olive oil, garlic, and mint and season generously. Leave to
   keep warm in the pan.

2. Bring a large pan of water to the boil with a couple of teaspoons of salt.
   When the water is boiling add the pasta. Three minutes before the pasta is
   ready (check timing instructions on the packet), add the broccoli. After
   another minute add the broad beans. After a further minute add the peas.
   A minute later the pasta and vegetables should be cooked. Check pasta,
   then drain.

3. Add the pasta and vegetables to the warm potato mixture. Stir well. Finally
   stir in the grated Parmesan, check the seasoning and serve.

WHOLE STRAWBERRY JAM

Anyone who lives near a pick-your-own farm will find themselves at some stage with too many strawberries on their hands. It is impossible to resist the urge to pick more than you need if you have row after row of luscious ripe fruit sitting in front of you. I first started on this over-picking tendency when I was very small and me and my best pal Claudie were left in a strawberry field by our parents, who came back to find they had to move into wholesale jam production. Unfortunately it was during a sugar shortage and my mother spent the next week pestering half the shopkeepers in the county for extra sugar.

I would therefore have liked to include a foolproof recipe for strawberry jam with whole strawberries in it. However, my experience as an adult is that getting strawberry jam to set is a tricky business, because strawberries are low in pectin. There are various strategies to get round this problem such as making pectin stock from apples or buying sugar with added pectin.

However, the important point as far as I'm concerned is that home-made strawberry jam which is technically unsuccessful (i.e. rather runny) is really delicious, and almost certainly nicer than virtually anything you can buy in a shop. So, here is an unreliable recipe for reliably delicious strawberry jam:

3 kg (6 lb) hulled strawberries
3 kg (6 lb) sugar
Juice of 2 lemons

1. Put the strawberries, sugar and lemon juice in a pan and heat gently until all the sugar has dissolved. Bring to the boil and boil rapidly until setting point is reached (or 20 minutes, whichever is the shorter) then leave to cool until a thin skin begins to set on its surface. Stir the jam gently to distribute the fruit and pour it into jars.

JULY

Summer salads

Lebanese plate: Baba ganoush, tabouleh with
roast peppers and green beans in a tomato and honey vinaigrette

Salad of roast Mediterranean vegetables and pasta,
Puy lentils in a truffled balsamic vinaigrette

Saintly sandwiches

Olive oil bread (for making the sandwiches with)

Hummus and roast pepper sandwich

Pesto and mozzarella with tomatoes, watercress and roast courgettes

Some other sandwich ideas

Summer supper

Pea, lettuce and mint soup

Carrot and coriander gateau with white wine and saffron sauce,
buttered spinach and new potatoes

Cherry strudel

Seasonal pleasure: making ice cream

Bridget's strawberry ice cream and tayberry variation

Apricot, honey and Amaretto iced yoghurt

Sarah's spiced vanilla ice cream

Cornish fairings (to serve with ice cream)

Summer salads

LEBANESE PLATE: BABA GANOUSH, TABOULEH WITH ROAST PEPPERS AND GREEN BEANS IN A TOMATO AND HONEY VINAIGRETTE

I can't guarantee that this is a completely authentic Lebanese collection, coming as it did via a New Zealand cook, but it is a very delicious and strongly flavoured plateful. If you haven't tasted proper baba ganoush (charred aubergine purée) this will be a real eye-opener for you.

You should certainly try to get hold of a bottle of Chateau Musar, a massively flavoursome Lebanese wine, which, like the figs described on page 196 is produced surrounded by missiles and armies. There must have been a gentleman's agreement not to bomb these vineyards.

Like most salads, all the parts of this dish are much more flavoursome if served at room temperature than straight from the fridge. The baba ganoush can happily be prepared the day before but should be brought back to room temperature before eating.

All parts of the Lebanese plate serve 6 as a main course when served in this combination.

Baba ganoush (charred aubergine purée)

This dish was a revelation to me. The combination of the smoky aubergine flavour with the utterly velvety texture is pure seductive luxury. There are people who don't like the resulting flavour, but they are in a sad minority. This is a very rich concoction so don't serve too much on each plate. You will probably find you don't eat all this quantity in one meal, but it keeps well in the fridge for a couple of days, and is great in sandwiches.

To make this dish properly you have to take your courage in both hands and burn the aubergines very thoroughly over an open flame.

> 800 g (1 lb 12 oz) aubergine (about 2 medium sized aubergines)
> 2 small cloves garlic, crushed
> 150 g (6 oz) pale tahini (about a half of a normal sized jar)
> Juice of 2 lemons
> 150 ml (5 fl oz) olive oil

1. Cook the aubergines over an open flame. This is most easily done on a gas hob, but could probably also be done with a fierce grill. The point is to char the skin completely. To achieve this properly will probably take about 10–15 minutes on a fierce gas flame, turning the aubergine as soon as each side is scorched and collapsed. Don't worry about going too far. It is virtually impossible to overdo the burning process.

2. Leave the charred aubergines to cool. When they are cool, gently remove the skin. You will find that little flecks of burnt skin remain. This is fine and will add to the flavour, but you want to get rid of all substantial bits of skin and the stalk.

3. Purée the peeled flesh with all the other ingredients in a food processor. Add some salt to taste.

Tabouleh with roast peppers

This tabouleh is made without garlic, as there is plenty in the other bits of this plate. Also, authentic tabouleh would not be frivolously decorated with roast peppers, but the combination works well in this plate, so why worry?

Some greengrocers sell parsley in very large bunches. If you have such a shop nearby, this is the recipe to take advantage of the fact. You cannot have too much parsley in tabouleh.

1 large red pepper, in fat strips
1 large yellow pepper, in fat strips
2 tbsp olive oil
Salt and pepper

225 g (8 oz) coarse bulghur wheat
(If you have fine bulghur you just need to soak it in boiling water, not actually cook it)
425 ml (¾ pint) water

3 tbsp olive oil
Juice of 1 lemon (more to taste)
1 bunch parsley, chopped (either curly or flat leaf is fine)
1 bunch mint, chopped

1. Pre-heat the oven to 230°C (450°F/Gas Mark 8). Roast the peppers in the olive oil and seasoning until they are just beginning to colour at the edges and their skin has gone wrinkly. Set aside.

2. Put the water and some salt in a pan with a closely fitting lid and bring to the boil. Add the bulghur and simmer for 5–10 minutes until all the water has been absorbed and the bulghur is chewy but cooked. Stir in the olive oil and allow to cool.

3. Mix the bulghur with all the other ingredients and serve in a gracious Lebanese manner.

Green beans in a tomato and honey vinaigrette

350 g fine beans, topped, tailed and halved

1 beef tomato, or two small plum tomatoes
1 tsp white wine vinegar
1 tsp honey
½ clove garlic, crushed
3 tbsp olive oil
Salt and freshly ground black pepper

1. Bring a pan of water to the boil and put in the beans. Simmer for about 5 minutes, then drain and plunge into cold water to stop them cooking any further. Drain again, very thoroughly this time.

2. De-seed and finely dice the tomatoes. Mix well with all the other ingredients including the beans. Season to taste.

SALAD OF ROAST MEDITERRANEAN VEGETABLES WITH PASTA, PUY LENTILS IN A TRUFFLED BALSAMIC VINAIGRETTE

Like tomatoes and basil, this is another classic Italian combination. It can be served either hot or at room temperature as a salad. If you are serving it as a salad you might want to toss a few rocket leaves in with the pasta and roast vegetables.

In both Hereford and at The Place Below we are always looking for summery and rich flavoured food that is vegetable rather than dairy based – much as I love good cheese, it's good to ring the changes. This dish has now become a firm favourite. In fact I made it for the only hen party I have ever attended.

We usually serve it with Puy lentils in a balsamic vinaigrette, but for added luxury (and a taste of what over-paid restaurant critics drone on about) add some truffle oil to the balsamic vinaigrette. Truffle oil (oil infused with either white or black truffles) is the only way that the amazing flavour of truffles is made accessible at anything other than vast prices. It is still a luxury item – a very small bottle (55 ml/2 fl oz) costs not a great deal less than £10 – but open the lid and give it a big sniff and you may find yourself with a costly new addiction. Don't on any account buy it in larger quantities, as you need very little of it to impart a strong flavour. Also, once you have opened a bottle, use it up as soon as possible, as the aroma seems to disappear quite quickly once the oil is exposed to air.

Of the two brands widely available in good Italian delicatessens, I would strongly recommend the Boscovivo brand called 'Condimento aromatizzato al tartufo' which comes in the above-mentioned 55 ml bottles rather than the one called 'Truffoil' or 'Truffoil light', both of which seem to have a much weaker smell of truffles.

The pasta

1 large aubergine, in chunks
1 red pepper, in thick strips
1 yellow pepper, in thick strips
2 medium courgettes, thickly sliced on the bias
125 ml (4 fl oz) olive oil
Salt and freshly ground black pepper

300 g (10 oz) dried penne pasta

1 bunch oregano (or marjoram) roughly chopped
1 bunch flat-leaved parsley, roughly chopped
1 tsp balsamic vinegar (or more to taste)
1 clove garlic, crushed

1. Pre-heat the oven to 230°C (450°F/Gas Mark 8). Roast the vegetables separately (*see instructions for roasting the vegetables in the Ratatouille on page 178*). The aubergine will take longest (perhaps half an hour), the peppers about 20 minutes, and the courgettes about 10–15 minutes. All these times will vary from oven to oven, however, so you have to do it largely by eye. The aubergine should be collapsed and golden, the peppers should be just colouring at the edges and beginning to go wrinkly, and the courgettes should be just taking on a little colour but still retain some firmness of texture.

2. When you put the courgettes in the oven, bring a large pan of salted water to the boil, and boil the pasta until just cooked. Drain and toss with the fresh herbs, balsamic vinegar, garlic and the roast vegetables, which should be just done if you're using 10 minute dried pasta.

The lentils

If you are serving these with the pasta, you should put the lentils on before you begin preparing your vegetables – but put the oven on first so that it can be heating up.

175 g (6 oz) Puy lentils
125 ml (4 fl oz) red wine
30 ml (1 fl oz) soy sauce
425 ml (15 fl oz) water

1 tbsp balsamic vinegar
1 tbsp olive oil
1 tbsp truffle oil
(If you can't get hold of truffle oil, just use double the quantity of olive oil)

1. Place the lentils in a pan with a well fitting lid together with the wine, soy sauce and water. Bring to the boil, turn down the heat and simmer with the lid on for about 35–45 minutes until the lentils are completely tender. Just about all of the liquid should have been absorbed. If it has not, turn up the heat and take the lid off the pan and boil fiercely until the remainder has evaporated or been absorbed.

2. Take off the heat and mix with the rest of the ingredients. Serve either at once or at room temperature.

Saintly sandwiches

OLIVE OIL BREAD
(FOR MAKING THE SANDWICHES WITH)

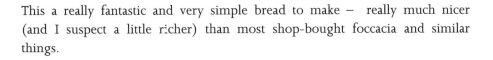

This a really fantastic and very simple bread to make – really much nicer (and I suspect a little richer) than most shop-bought foccacia and similar things.

We have experimented in both London and Hereford with various ways of making it. Professional bakers and the more academic baking books recommend that you first make a 'sponge' with all the water and the flour and then have a second mixing when you add the oil and the rest of the flour. We have found these complications to be unnecessary.

As well as being wonderful for the sandwich ideas given on the following pages, it is also the perfect accompaniment to minestrone-type soups.

As bread, it needs to be eaten on the day you make it – certainly no more than one day later. But it does freeze well, and also makes excellent toast, breadcrumbs and giant croutons if you have some going stale.

It's a useful rule of thumb that bread not only tastes best, but also that the chemistry of its growth works best, when you have approximately 2% of the weight of flour in salt. Less salt and the structure of the bread will be too spongy, more salt and the yeast is gradually killed and the dough over-toughened. (If you find the technical side of food and cookery remotely interesting, buy *On Food and Cooking* by Harold McGee, one of the most thumbed books on my shelf.)

1 kg (2 lb) strong white flour
20 g (generous ½ oz) sea salt
2 sachets easy blend yeast
700 ml (1¼ pints) water
100 ml (3½ fl oz) olive oil

1. Put the dry ingredients in a large mixing bowl and mix briefly.

2. Gradually add the water and the oil (either together or separately, it does not matter) mixing with a large spoon as you go. When the dough is roughly mixed you have to plunge in with your hand. This is a very wet and sticky dough, but don't add more flour or you will lose the character-istic loose and bubbly texture of the finished bread. You need to use your hand as a dough hook, scraping the dough from the bottom of the bowl with a motion that is half mixing, half kneading. You will feel the sticky mass gradually transformed into a still sticky but coherent elastic blob. This should take about 10 minutes of vigorous mixing/kneading. (If you have a mixer with a dough hook, you simply switch it on and go and have a cup of coffee, which is easier.)

3. When making the bread at the restaurants, we usually put the dough in the fridge overnight at this point. This has the advantage that the dough is easier to roll out when it is cold, but is not otherwise necessary.

4. Pre-heat the oven to 240°C (475°F/Gas Mark 9). Oil a deep, very large, baking tray 46cm x 36cm (18" x 14") or two ordinary large ones.

5. Generously flour a worktop and pin and roll the dough into approximately the shape of the tin (or tins). If you are not used to rolling out bread dough, you may find this quite challenging the first couple of times you do it. Use plenty of flour and don't worry. The bread will taste good and it's supposed to be rustic anyway. When the dough is rolled out, roll it back onto the pin and unroll it into the tin. Pull and push it as necessary to get it into the corners.

6. Leave it to rise until it looks puffy and risen – this may take between 45 minutes and 2½ hours depending on the temperature and the kitchen. If you are uncertain, leave it a bit longer.

7. Put in the oven for about 20 minutes, turning the loaf halfway through if your oven cooks more quickly in one part than in another. Turn out to cool on a wire rack.

We get 12 large sandwiches out of each loaf.

HUMMUS AND ROAST PEPPER SANDWICH

This sandwich, although packed with rich flavours, is made without using any dairy produce – which just goes to show that good food can be both delicious and good for you.

MAKES 6 VERY LARGE SANDWICHES

2 medium red or yellow peppers, de-seeded and cut into thick strips
2 red onions, cut into wedges
3 tbsp extra virgin olive oil

400 g (14 oz) can of chickpeas, drained (keep the liquid)
(or 200 g/7 oz soaked, drained and cooked)
1 tbsp pale tahini paste
1 tsp salt
Juice of 1 lemon
½ garlic clove, crushed
5 tbsp extra virgin olive oil
Seasoning

Olive oil bread – half a large loaf (see page 133)

40 g (1½ oz) bag rocket

1. Preheat the oven to 230°C(450°F/Gas Mark 8). Toss the peppers and onions in the oil. Season and spread on the baking tray. Place in the oven for about 20–25 minutes until the skins of the peppers are just beginning to colour and the onions are starting to caramelise.

2. To make the hummus, place all the ingredients except the olive oil in a food processor. Add 3 tablespoons of the reserved liquid from the chick-peas and process until smooth. With the motor still running, pour in the olive oil. If it is too thick add a little more of the reserved cooking liquor. Season.

3. Cut the half loaf of olive oil bread into six squares and split each in half horizontally. Spread hummus on the bottom halves. Top with the roasted peppers, onions, rocket and seasoning. Sandwich with the top of the bread.

PESTO AND MOZZARELLA WITH TOMATOES, WATERCRESS AND ROAST COURGETTES

This has been one of our most popular sandwiches at All Saints. The only secrets to its deliciousness are using home-made bread and home-made pesto.

For six people, slice a couple of medium sized courgettes 2 cm (1 inch) thick diagonally, toss in some seasoned olive oil and roast in a hot oven (230°C/450°F/Gas Mark 8) for about 10 minutes until just beginning to colour on the cut surfaces but still a little firm. Meanwhile spread both halves of the split olive oil bread (cut the same way as for the hummus sandwich above) with pesto and put a couple of slices of mozzarella (buffalo mozzarella if you are feeling extravagant) on top and a couple of slices of ripe tomato on top of that. As soon as the courgettes are ready put them on top with a few watercress leaves and complete with the top half of the sandwich.

You can also serve it all hot. After spreading the pesto put the two halves of the sandwich separately in the oven for 5 minutes. Take them out and put the mozzarella and tomato on. Put them back in the oven for a couple of minutes – enough to warm but not cook the mozzarella and tomato. Take them out again and top with the roast courgettes and watercress. Put the top on the sandwich and serve.

SOME OTHER SANDWICH IDEAS

Roast tofu and mushroom

Cut some firm plain tofu (Cauldron is the most widely available brand) into large thin squares (about the size of the sandwich and 1 cm thick) and marinate for a couple of hours in a mixture of equal quantities of soy sauce and red wine with some crushed garlic and ginger. Take them out of the marinade and turn them in sesame oil mixed with tabasco. Spread them out on a baking sheet and roast in a hot oven for about 30 minutes or until they are going crisp on the outside. Meanwhile, brush the gills of some large field mushrooms with olive oil, garlic and a little salt and pepper. Roast the mushrooms in a hot oven for about 10 minutes until they have begun to give off their juice. Arrange the tofu and field mushrooms one on top of the other in the sandwich and garnish with some salad leaves.

Tapenade with roast sweet potato and fresh goat's cheese

I've already mentioned the delicious fresh goat's cheese made by Neal's Yard Creamery just outside Hereford. As well as using it in quiches, we use it in partnership with roast sweet potatoes with great success both in salads and sandwiches. Cut the sweet potato into long strips about 1cm thick and roast in seasoned olive oil until very tender and colouring at the edges. Purée some good olives with a little garlic and a few capers. Spread this mixture on the bread instead of butter and top with the roast sweet potato and fresh, creamy goat's cheese.

Two winter warming sandwiches

The recipe for Warm Brie and Plum Sandwich can be found on page 186.

Another fantastic fruit and cheese combination is roast pear and Stilton. Cut some pears into quarters and toss in a little melted butter and sugar. Spread on a baking sheet and roast in a hot oven until the pears are just tender. Heat buttered bread in the oven until crisp. Put the slices back in the oven with the roast pear on one half and some crumbled Stilton on the other half. Leave in the oven for about a minute until the Stilton is beginning to melt. Put the two halves together – with some rocket or watercress if you have some – and serve.

Summer supper

PEA, LETTUCE AND MINT SOUP

A simple mixture of summer flavours.

50 g (2 oz) butter
350 g (12 oz) onions, diced
500 g (1 lb) potatoes, diced
1.25 litres (2 pints) water
750 g (1½ lb) peas (weight before shelling), shelled
2 round lettuces, taken apart
200 ml (7 fl oz) crème fraîche
Handful of mint leaves, roughly chopped
Scant juice of half a lemon

1. Sweat the onions in the butter until soft.

2. Add the potatoes and water. Bring to the boil and simmer until the potatoes are soft.

3. Add the peas and lettuce and simmer for a further 10 minutes.

4. Take off the heat. Add the crème fraîche, mint and half the lemon juice. Blend and taste and season with more lemon juice, salt and pepper as necessary.

CARROT AND CORIANDER GATEAU WITH WHITE WINE AND SAFFRON SAUCE, BUTTERED SPINACH AND NEW POTATOES

This is a dish which raises the humble carrot to really fine levels.

Serve it with the White Wine and Tarragon Sauce on page 72 but substitute some powdered saffron for the tarragon. For the buttered spinach, briefly boil 1 kg (2 lb) of spinach. Drain it thoroughly. Heat a good knob of butter and turn the spinach in it until it is hot. Season with salt, pepper and freshly grated nutmeg.

SERVES 6

1 kg (2 lb) carrots, chopped into large chunks
75 g (3 oz) butter

100 g (4 oz) Parmesan, grated
2 tbsp coriander seeds, roasted and ground
200 ml (7 fl oz) single cream
2 eggs

1. Pre-heat the oven to 190°C (375°F/Gas Mark 5).

2. Sweat the carrots in the butter and some salt – but not for too long. The carrots should have lost their crunchiness but still be quite firm.

3. Put the carrots in the blender and pulse briefly so that the carrots are not puréed but chopped into very small pieces. (Alternatively, you could chop them into small pieces by hand.)

4. Mix the Parmesan, coriander, cream and eggs and stir in the finely chopped carrots. Check the seasoning.

5. Butter six individual 200 ml (7 fl oz) aluminium dariole moulds and divide the mixture between them. Put them into a deep baking dish and pour water in to half way up the dariole moulds to create a bain-marie. Put in the oven for about 45 minutes until set. Allow to rest for 10 minutes, run a knife around the edge, turn the gateau out and serve. Or, if you want to make them in advance, turn them out of their moulds once they have cooled a little and then return to the oven for 10 minutes or so to re-heat just before you want to eat.

CHERRY STRUDEL

The cherry season is short, and unlike many seasonal fruits, cherries never become really cheap. The result is that we cook with them relatively infrequently. For this excellent recipe, we have found that frozen cherries (which have the advantage of being already pitted) work very well. The idea comes from Anton Mosimann via Jane Grigson's wonderful Fruit Book.

SERVES 8

50 g (2 oz) breadcrumbs
20 g (1 oz) pine kernels
50 g (2 oz) hazelnuts, toasted and then finely ground
50 g (2 oz) butter, melted
1 kg (2 lb) stoned cherries (frozen is fine)
125 g (4 oz) caster sugar
25 g (1 oz) cinnamon
100 g (4 oz) sultanas

275 g (10 oz) filo pastry

1. Preheat oven to 180°C (350°F/Gas Mark 4).

2. Mix the breadcrumbs with the pine nuts and ground hazelnuts.

3. Melt the butter.

4. Mix the cherries with the sugar, cinnamon and sultanas. (Note: if using frozen cherries they should be thoroughly drained first – retain the juice and make a sauce out of it.)

5. Arrange the filo pastry so that you have a very large oblong, buttering between each layer, with four sheets just overlapping to form each layer, thoroughly buttering each sheet as you go. Continue again until the pastry is three layers thick.

6. Sprinkle the nut mixture over the pastry, leaving a 2 cm (1 inch) border, and then brush some more melted butter over the nut mixture.

7. Spread the cherry mixture on top.

8. Starting from the longest edge, wrap up like a roly-poly and put on a baking sheet. Butter the outside thoroughly.

9. Bake in the pre-heated oven for about 35 minutes until brown and crisp. Leave to cool a little before slicing. Serve with crème fraîche or clotted cream.

Seasonal pleasure: making ice cream

BRIDGET'S STRAWBERRY ICE CREAM AND TAYBERRY VARIATION

Every summer Sarah waxes lyrical about a simple strawberry ice cream which her mother Bridget used to make, so this year I thought I would try to make it to see if it was all it was cracked up to be. I must say that it is delicious – and provided great comfort when eaten with Cornish Fairings (*see page 150*) the night Sarah failed to teach me the tune to 'there's only one Michael Owen...' and England got knocked out of the 1998 World Cup. As well as Bridget's version (which she tells me comes from Mrs Beeton) I make an even simpler version which is basically frozen strawberry fool. If you're comfortable making custards then the Mrs Beeton version is smoother and more sophisticated, but the other is also really delicious.

As with the other ice cream recipes in this book, these two don't require an ice cream machine. You just have to remember to fork them from time to time in the deep freeze to prevent the build up of ice crystals.

The quantities for the tayberry ice cream give a more sorbet-like confection, but either recipe could be used for either fruit or for raspberries. The tayberry quantities have a greater tendency to form ice crystals, so more regular and energetic forking is required.

Each recipe makes plenty for six people.

Mrs Beeton's (and Bridget's) strawberry ice cream

SERVES 6

300 ml (10 fl oz) double cream
150 ml (5 fl oz) milk
2 egg yolks
175 g (6 oz) caster sugar
500 g (1 lb) strawberries, hulled
1 tsp lemon juice

1. Bring milk and cream to boiling point. Off the heat, add the beaten egg yolks and stir until the mixture thickens, then add sugar. When dissolved, strain (don't bother unless you've got lumps) and cool.

2. Pass the strawberries through a fine sieve, mix with the custard, add lemon juice and freeze. Fork thoroughly after one hour, put back in the freezer and fork again after a further hour. Leave for several more hours or overnight to solidify. Serve with Cornish Fairings (*see page 150*).

Even simpler strawberry ice cream

375 g (12 oz) strawberries, hulled
100 g (4 oz) caster sugar
300 ml (10 fl oz) double cream

See overleaf for method.

Even simpler tayberry ice cream

We picked loads of tayberries from a local pick your own last year. They seem to survive a rather wet summer better than some other soft fruit.

500 g (1 lb) tayberries
75 g (3 oz) sugar
200 ml (7 fl oz) double cream

The method is the same for both ice creams.

1. Mash the fruit and sugar thoroughly.

2. Whip the cream to soft peaks.

3. Fold the cream into the fruit purée and put in a plastic container in the deep freeze.

4. After about one and a half hours, take the ice cream out and bash it around vigorously with a large fork, concentrating on those bits which have begun to solidify. Repeat this process an hour later and then after a further hour. Then leave it for several more hours or overnight to solidify.

APRICOT, HONEY AND AMARETTO ICED YOGHURT

There is quite a generous slug of Amaretto in this. If you are not so keen on the almondy flavour of Amaretto (actually made from the kernels of apricot and so particularly appropriate as a pairing for apricots) then you could use brandy, or a bit less Amaretto, or nothing at all – there is plenty of flavour in this without the booze.

Redcurrant sauce makes a lovely accompaniment to this ice cream. Cook some redcurrants briefly with a bit of sugar to taste, and strain. If it's too thick, add a very small amount of water.

These quantities make a large batch which serves at least 12, but if you are going to the trouble of making your own ice cream you are much better off making a decent-sized batch, and it takes no more time to make double the quantity.

250 g (8 oz) dried apricots
300 ml (10 fl oz) water
100 ml (3 fl oz) Amaretto
2 generous dessertspoons of runny honey (about 100 g/4 oz)
450 g (1 lb) full fat Greek yoghurt
100 ml (4 fl oz) double cream

1. Put the dried apricots and water in a lidded pan and bring to the boil. Simmer for about 40 minutes until the apricots are very tender and most of the water has been absorbed. The time and amount of water needed will vary depending on how dried the apricots are.

2. Put the cooked apricots and any remaining cooking liquor together with all the other ingredients in a blender and whizz until very smooth.

3. Put in a freezer-proof plastic container and put in the freezer for 4–6 hours until completely frozen, forking thoroughly every 1–1½ hours.

4. Take out of the freezer 10–15 minutes before you want to eat it to make it easier to serve.

SARAH'S SPICED VANILLA ICE CREAM

Fancy bits of kitchen equipment such as ice cream makers often come with little cookery books or leaflets. Generally, these are thoroughly awful, but the one which we got with our ice cream maker we actually use much more often than the ice cream maker itself. I rang up the manufacturer and complained that the machine wasn't working properly, and they pointed out that the custard (which is the basis of most ice creams) needs to be chilled before you put it into the machine. Now if you are going to chill the custard anyway, why not freeze it straight away and just remember to fork it every hour or two – and then you don't have an ice cream maker to clean?

Anyway, this recipe is slightly adapted from the excellent *Ice Creams and Sorbets* by Jacki Passmore (Salamander Books) which came with our machine.

I used to have another good line about this recipe: 'My wife only cooks spiced vanilla ice cream.' However, since the arrival of our son Jonathan, she doesn't even cook ice cream. You just can't get the staff these days.

SERVES 12

500 ml (18 fl oz) whole milk
1 cinnamon stick
3 whole green cardamoms, broken
3 cm (1½ inch) piece of fresh root ginger, peeled and chopped up fine
4 whole cloves
2 star anise
A generous scraping of nutmeg

8 egg yolks
200 g (7 oz) sugar
2 tsp real vanilla essence
750 ml (1¼ pints) double cream

1. In a small saucepan, simmer milk with spices for 30 minutes. Let it stand until it is cool and then strain through a fine sieve.

2. In a medium sized, heavy-bottomed pan whisk the egg yolks and sugar over a very low heat until thick and creamy.

3. Scald the cream and strained milk with vanilla. Pour onto the beaten egg and sugar mixture and continue cooking on a very low heat for about 10 minutes until the custard thickens. Put in a covered plastic container and freeze for 4–6 hours, forking very thoroughly every 1–1½ hours. Before serving, refrigerate for 20 minutes or so to soften.

CORNISH FAIRINGS

Great with ice cream.

I found this recipe in a Cornish cookery booklet by Ann Pascoe and I was delighted to find that they come out looking exactly like the biscuits that you buy in touristy tins with pictures of Cornish views, but taste rather better. They are basically crunchy, just a little bit chewy and with a fairly hefty kick of ginger. I've made the kick even more hefty by adding some stem ginger.

Sometimes I melt a little chocolate and, using a dessertspoon, just drizzle it over each biscuit in a wiggledy pattern. This more luxurious version is a great biscuit to have around over Christmas as well.

Makes about 24 biscuits

250 g (8 oz) plain white flour
½ tsp salt
2 tsp baking powder
2 tsp bicarbonate of soda
3 tsp mixed spice
3 tsp ground ginger
2 blobs stem ginger (from a jar in syrup), very finely diced

125 g (4 oz) butter
125 g (4 oz) caster sugar
200 g (7 oz) golden syrup

(optional extra: 75 g (3 oz) chocolate, melted and drizzled over the finished biscuits)

1. Put the dry ingredients (flour, salt, baking powder, bicarbonate of soda, mixed spice, ground ginger) in a food processor and whizz briefly. Add the butter and whizz again until there is a breadcrumby texture. Add the sugar and whizz again.

2. Warm the golden syrup a little so that it is runny, add the syrup and stem ginger to the processor and whizz again.

3. You can either make the biscuits straight away or leave the mixture in the fridge until you are ready to make them.

4. Preheat the oven to 180°C (350°F/Gas Mark 4).

5. Roll the biscuit mixture into walnut sized balls and space them out very well on a baking sheet lined with baking parchment. I only fit eight biscuits onto a large 46 cm x 36 cm (18" x 14") catering baking sheet so you will probably only get about five on a typical large domestic baking sheet.

6. Bake for about 12 minutes until they are golden all over then take out of the oven. If your oven cooks more quickly on the top shelf then move the biscuits to the bottom shelf after about 8 minutes, or as soon as they begin to brown. You may also find, if you are re-using the same baking sheet for successive batches, that the biscuits cook increasingly quickly as the baking sheet heats up. They can take as little as 8 minutes by the end of a batch.

7. Allow to cool for a few minutes on the baking sheet before removing to finish cooling on a wire rack. Store in an airtight container.

AUGUST

August bank holiday dinner

Chilled cucumber, sorrel and avocado soup

Cashew and lentil pâté with cantaloupe melon, peaches,
avocado and a chilli and lime vinaigrette

Pesto summer pudding (courgette and tomatoes)
served with a leaf and herb salad

Roast nectarines with raspberry sauce and crème fraîche

Seasonal pleasures

Potatoes – the ultimate potato salad recipe

Tomatoes

Elderberries – elderberry vinegar

Plums – plum jam

August bank holiday dinner

CHILLED CUCUMBER, SORREL AND AVOCADO SOUP

This is a classic summer soup adapted from a couple of different ideas in Lindsay Bareham's excellent *Soup Book*.

2 tbsp sunflower oil
200 g (8 oz) leeks, chopped
1 cucumber, peeled and roughly chopped
1 tbsp cornmeal
1 litre water

150 g (5 oz) sorrel, roughly chopped
2 ripe avocados
175 g (6 oz) Greek yoghurt

1. In a medium sized pan, soften the leeks in the sunflower oil.

2. Add the peeled and chopped cucumber and continue sweating for about 5 minutes.

3. Add the cornmeal and water. Bring to the boil and simmer for 10 minutes. Take the pan off the heat and allow to cool a little. Purée with the sorrel, avocados and Greek yoghurt.

4. Chill thoroughly before serving. To stop the top of the soup going brown (because of the avocado), cover it with clingfilm while storing in the fridge.

CASHEW AND LENTIL PÂTÉ WITH CANTALOUPE MELON, PEACHES, AVOCADO AND A CHILLI AND LIME VINAIGRETTE

This is a dish that we often serve as a main course in the summer at The Place Below, and is adapted from a Sarah Brown idea. A slightly smaller portion makes, as here, an excellent starter. There are two things that can make this pâté not simply 'unusual' (always a two-edged comment) but also totally delicious and just what you want to eat on a hot August day. First, be sure to season the pâté well, as lentils (and pulses generally) need plenty of salt. Secondly, don't even think about eating this unless you have got really ripe fruit. It doesn't have to be the fruit specified, but whatever it is (really good mangoes and papaya are also excellent), they must be in prime condition. Melons are one of the things that many of us have ceased to treat as seasonal, but have a look in late August and September and you will almost certainly find melons abundant, cheap, and, if you are careful in your selection and storage at home, really delicious.

The pâté can be made a day or two in advance and stored in the fridge. The fruit should be peeled and prepared as short a time as possible before you eat. For the most elegant presentation, keep your chunks of fruit large.

100 g (4 oz) red lentils
1 tsp sunflower oil
1 medium onion finely chopped
1 tsp ground cumin
½ tsp ground turmeric
½ tsp ground coriander
½ tsp wholegrain mustard
2 tbsp smooth peanut butter
Juice of one lemon
100 g (4 oz) cashew nuts, toasted and finely chopped

½ tsp chilli powder
Salt and freshly ground black pepper

1 lime, juice and zest
¼ large red chilli, de-seeded and very finely chopped
1 bunch fresh mint
4 tbsp sunflower oil

1 ripe cantaloupe melon, peeled, de-seeded and cut into long, thick strips
3 peaches, peeled, stoned and cut into six
2 ripe avocados, peeled, stoned and cut into six

1. Place the lentils in a pan with 250 ml (9 fl oz) water and simmer with the lid on for about 15 minutes until the lentils are soft and the water is absorbed. (If they are not quite soft but all the water is gone, add a little more water and keep on cooking.)

2. Meanwhile, heat the oil in a pan, add the onion, spices and mustard and cook for about 5 minutes until the onions are soft. Add to the lentils with the peanut butter, lemon juice, nuts, chilli and seasoning. Mix well and taste for sufficient seasoning. Don't be shy of adding plenty more salt if it needs it. Transfer to a container and chill until ready to use.

3. For the dressing, place the lime juice and zest, diced chilli and mint in a blender and whizz until smooth. With the blender still running, add the oil slowly until incorporated, and season.

4. Prepare the fruit.

5. To serve, make three quenelles (technical term for almond-shaped blobs) of the pâté for each person and arrange like the spokes of a wheel in the middle of a large plate. Arrange the bits of fruit between them (as additional spokes of the wheel) and dribble some dressing over the top. Eat.

PESTO SUMMER PUDDING (COURGETTE AND TOMATOES) SERVED WITH A LEAF AND HERB SALAD

This is a really delicious and pretty dish. However, don't bother making it unless you are using Home-made Pesto (*see page xiii*) and can get hold of decent little tomatoes. You can sometimes buy Gardeners' Delight at supermarkets (*see page 162 for a tomato discussion*), and now baby plum tomatoes are becoming increasingly available which are also fine for this. Out of season cherry tomatoes tend to be very disappointing in flavour.

Serve with boiled new potatoes and some mixed leaves tossed in a mint and parsley vinaigrette.

SERVES 6

1 medium sliced white loaf
Olive oil
Salt and pepper

250 g (8 oz) courgettes, quartered lengthways and thickly sliced
150 g (6 oz) cherry tomatoes (preferably Gardeners' Delight), halved
150 g (6 oz) pesto

1. Pre-heat the oven to 230°C (450°F/Gas Mark 8).

2. Cut the crusts off the bread. Brush 6 individual dariole moulds lightly with olive oil. Brush the bread with olive oil and season with salt and pepper. Line the tins with the bread, making sure there are no gaps.

3. Blanch the courgettes for a minute in boiling water and drain. Mix with the halved cherry tomatoes and the pesto. Fill the lined moulds with the mixture. Put a lid of bread on and brush with seasoned olive oil. Bake for about 15–20 minutes in a very hot oven until golden on top.

4. To serve: Dress some mixed leaves and herbs (e.g. dill, flat parsley, mint) and arrange all over a plate leaving a hole in the middle. Arrange some boiled new potatoes dressed in a little olive oil and lemon around the salad. When the puddings are cooked, carefully ease them out of the moulds (they should be golden on the outside) and put in the middle of the plate.

ROAST NECTARINES WITH RASPBERRY SAUCE AND CRÈME FRAÎCHE

Delicious autumn raspberries are gradually becoming readily available and they make a natural partner for nectarines.

SERVES 6

6 nectarines
50 g (2 oz) butter
2 tsp runny honey
1 tbsp slivered almonds

150 g (6 oz) raspberries
25 g (1 oz) sugar
Crème fraîche

1. Pre-heat the oven to 240°C (475°F/Gas Mark 9).

2. Butter a baking dish. Halve and stone the nectarines and arrange them skin side down in the bottom of the dish. Put a little knob of butter in the middle of each nectarine half and then a drop of runny honey and a light sprinkling of slivered almonds.

3. Put in the oven for 15 minutes.

4. Meanwhile, gently warm the raspberries with the sugar until the raspberries are going mushy. Pass the sauce through a chinoise or sieve and taste for sweetness.

5. Serve the hot nectarines with a dollop of the sauce and a blob of crème fraîche.

Seasonal pleasures: potatoes, tomatoes, elderberries, plum jam

THE ULTIMATE POTATO SALAD RECIPE

As I said earlier, one of the biggest successes of my first year of vegetable growing was Charlotte potatoes. They have a lovely waxy texture and, especially when they are quite new, a lovely earthy flavour. You really need a waxy salad potato to make this salad as good as it should be. Charlottes and Rattes are the most commonly sold in supermarkets; if you're lucky you might find Pink Fir Apples in a good specialist greengrocer. And if you run a café in Hereford you occasionally get Pink Fir Apples delivered by Mrs Mason all beautifully washed! All of them tend to be significantly more expensive than ordinary potatoes, but they really make a difference in this kind of dish.

I would describe this dressing as an almond and roast garlic mayonnaise except that there are no eggs in it. It is a dressing which is more easily made in larger quantities – the quantities given here would probably dress about 2 kg (5 lb) of new potatoes.

FULL QUANTITY OF SAUCE (USE ONLY HALF FOR A BIT MORE THAN A KILO OF POTATOES)

140 g (5 oz) garlic (2 medium sized bulbs)
60 g (2 oz) ground almonds
1 tsp salt
90 ml (3 fl oz) water
1 tbsp white wine vinegar
300 ml sunflower oil

1. Pre-heat the oven to 230°C (450°F/Gas Mark 8).

2. Break the garlic bulbs into cloves, but do not peel, and spread them out onto a baking sheet. Bake for 10–15 minutes until soft when pressed and smelling toasty. Allow to cool and then peel.

3. Toast the ground almonds, either in the oven, spreading them out on a baking sheet, and turning over after about 5 minutes when the ones on the surface are coloured, or in a dry pan over a medium heat, stirring every 30 seconds or so until most are golden coloured. Allow to cool.

4. Put the peeled baked garlic and the toasted almonds in a blender together with the salt, water and vinegar and whizz until very smooth. While still whizzing gradually pour in the sunflower oil. Check the seasoning and pour over recently boiled potatoes.

TOMATOES

The supermarkets have given us all a good laugh in the last couple of years with their introduction of new varieties which are 'grown for flavour'. What were they grown for before? Well, of course, the answer is easy transportation, large yields and cheapness.

You do occasionally see the king of tomatoes – Gardeners' Delight, a truly wonderful but low-yielding cherry tomato – for sale in supermarkets. They still don't taste quite like the home-grown item, which will be ripening by the end of August. At their best these are sweet enough to eat like fruit and with that delicious aroma of freshly picked tomato.

So look out for really ripe looking tomatoes at this time of year. If you can find ripe Marmande tomatoes (the very uneven large tomatoes) then simply slice them, pour decent olive oil over them, season generously, and scatter a few torn basil leaves on top. Eat with the Olive Oil Bread (*see page* 133).

If you find ripe plum tomatoes then make the simple pasta recipe described on page 81.

If you have a glut of any good tomatoes, cut them in half and lay out to dry on large baking sheets in a very low oven for about 4 hours, until there is no surface liquid. Put in a container with olive oil and garlic; they are incredibly useful for quick pasta and pizzas.

For a variation on traditional stuffed tomatoes: scoop the insides out of some good-sized beef tomatoes. Make a risotto using the insides of the tomatoes, wild rice, some red wine, water, a few re-hydrated dried tomatoes with their soaking liquor and a little soy sauce. Wild rice cooks very slowly when cooked in a thick stock like this, so allow plenty of time. Stuff the tomatoes with the risotto and serve with a little Pesto (*see page* xiii) or a cashew and basil cream. For the cashew and basil cream: Grind raw cashews to a powder, add a little water and blend. Add more water, boil, simmer and blend again. Add a good bunch of basil, blend yet again, season and re-heat and serve warm with the stuffed tomatoes.

ELDERBERRIES

Elderflower cordial has made a great comeback over the last few years and there are several decent brands readily available. However, despite their easy availability, elderberries are not much used. You get a lot of pip compared with fruit, and the flavour, although very pleasant, is quite mild.

My mother used to make elderberry dessert jelly and elderberry and apple crumble, both of which we used to enjoy. Sarah and I have had great success with two elderberry recipes: elderberry and apple jelly in the style of redcurrant jelly, which is quite a palaver to make, and a delicious spiced elderberry vinegar which we found in the pages of BBC *Vegetarian Good Food* magazine. It makes a sweet vinegar which combines beautifully with walnut oil to enliven winter salads. I have no doubt that blackberries, which also tend to come into season in the second half of August, could be used to make a variation on this theme.

Spiced elderberry vinegar

350 g (12 oz) elderberries, de-stalked
1 tsp cloves
1 cinnamon stick
½ tsp peppercorns (black or white)
300 ml (½ pint) white wine vinegar
175 g (6 oz) sugar

1. Put the elderberries and spices in a pan and cover with water. Bring to the boil and simmer for 20 minutes. Set aside until cold and then strain into a clean stainless steel pan.

2. Add the vinegar and sugar and heat gently until the sugar has dissolved. Boil and then simmer for 10 minutes until the liquid is very slightly thickened. Bottle and don't use for at least one month. Keeps for at least a year – we are still happily using the batch we made 15 months ago.

PLUM JAM

In the first year in which we lived in Herefordshire, August and September brought a glut of plums. The plum trees in our garden produced a mass of Victoria-like plums and various untended trees down the lane were laden with a darker purple-skinned fruit. We made batch after batch of plum jam, masses of plum chutney and some fantastic (but more labour-intensive) damson cheese. When our local W.I. chutney maker (I hadn't realised before that men were taking over the W.I.) in Hereford temporarily can't produce as much as we need for our sandwiches and ploughman's at the Café then I bring in a few jars from our still massive plum chutney stocks.

For all jam-making recipes my first port of call is the excellent and thorough *Home Preservation of Fruit and Vegetables* (HMSO). However, after making the first batch of jam in the recommended way, we thereafter skipped the step which involves adding blanched, skinned and halved plum stone kernels. However much it appeals as an idea to use absolutely all of the fruit, this is a mighty laborious task and I couldn't taste any significant difference in the final result.

This, then, is the simplified recipe.

2.75 kg (6 lb) plums, preferably either Victorias, or a green or yellow plum
300–900 ml (½ — 1½ pints) water
2.75 kg (6 lb) sugar

1. Wash, halve and stone the fruit.

2. Place the plums and water in the pan, adding about 300 ml (½ pint) of water and topping up as necessary during cooking.

3. Bring to the boil then simmer gently until the fruit is tender and the contents of the pan are greatly reduced.

4. Add the sugar and stir until it has dissolved, then bring to a rolling boil and boil hard until setting point has been reached.

If the plum variety you're using doesn't stone easily when raw, then stew them whole and allow to cool after they have softened. Roll your sleeves up and fish out the stones by hand, which is such a sensuous experience perhaps it should be done in any event. Reheat, reduce further if necessary, and proceed with stage 4.

See the marmalade recipe on page 19 for guidance on testing for the setting point and sterilizing jars.

SEPTEMBER

The month of harvest, and therefore a focal month of the year for people who like food.

Harvest supper 1: posh and delicious

Aubergine with truffle oil, Parmesan and rocket

Clear field mushroom and coriander soup

Nori sausages with pepperonata and arame

Hazelnut meringue cake with raspberry sauce

Harvest supper 2: simple and delicious

Corn on the cob with butter

Ratatouille with Asian flavours and roast tofu

Ian's spiced chickpeas

Bulghur with olive oil and lime

Blackberry and apple crumble

Seasonal pleasure: autumn fruits

Blackberries and autumn raspberries – Raspberry and apple cake

Grapes

Plums – warm Brie on toast with plum compote

Harvest supper 1: posh and delicious

AUBERGINE WITH TRUFFLE OIL, PARMESAN AND ROCKET

I think this is a really special dish — the aubergines providing maximum surface area from which the smell of truffle oil can waft up to you (for more information about truffle oil see page 130). Do not chill the aubergines after cooking them — this dish must be served at room temperature.

SERVES 6

3 large aubergines
175 ml (6 fl oz) olive oil
Salt and pepper
A very small bottle of truffle oil
A couple of handfuls of rocket
Block of Parmesan for shaving
1 lemon for garnish

1. Pre-heat the oven to 220°C (425°F).

2. Slice the aubergines into six lengthways (into slices about 1cm (⅓ inch) thick). Brush each side with olive oil seasoned with salt and freshly ground pepper. Place the aubergine slices onto baking sheets with none overlapping. Bake in the oven until golden on both sides, turning the pieces over after about 10 minutes so that they cook evenly. Set on one side.

3. To serve, lay three bits of aubergine on a large plate and brush the upper surface lightly with truffle oil. Shave some Parmesan over. Scatter some rocket randomly on top. Garnish with a wedge of lemon.

CLEAR FIELD MUSHROOM
AND CORIANDER SOUP

This is my wife's favourite soup. I made it first after we ate something similar at the excellent Museum Street Café – a marvellous restaurant where, like us, they produce a great deal of very fresh food from a tiny kitchen.

This is a strongly flavoured but light soup, with plenty of field mushrooms (don't substitute button or chestnut mushrooms) backed up with the stock made from one of the most delicious store cupboard ingredients – dried cepes (also sold as porcini, the Italian name). You may find an inferior and cheaper mixture of dried wild mushrooms for sale called something like melange de foret – I wouldn't bother with them.

There is a lot of potential for grit in this soup. Be sure to strain the liquid from the soaked dried cepes carefully, and also to wash the coriander thoroughly – it often seems to arrive in the shops dirtier than other herbs.

60 g (2 oz) dried *cepes/porcini*
(for some reason never sold under their English name of Penny Buns)
1.5 litres (2¾ pints) *hot water*

2 tbsp *sunflower oil*
1 medium *onion, finely chopped*
2 cm (1 inch) *root ginger, finely chopped*
2 cloves *garlic, crushed*
½ a small *medium strength chilli, seeds removed, finely chopped*
700 g (1½ lb) *field mushrooms, sliced about 1 cm thick*
Salt and freshly ground black pepper

150 ml (5 fl oz) *dry sherry or dry Madeira*
2 tbsp *dark soy sauce*
1 tbsp *balsamic vinegar*
1 tsp *sugar*
1 bunch *fresh coriander, roughly chopped*

1. Soak the dried mushrooms in the hot water for 20–30 minutes.

2. In a large pan, sweat the onion, ginger, garlic and chilli in the sunflower oil until the onions are soft (about 10 minutes). Add the mushrooms and a generous pinch of salt and continue cooking over a medium heat for about a further 10 minutes until the mushrooms have wilted and begun to give off their juice.

3. Strain the liquid from the soaking mushrooms through a fine sieve to take out any grit and add to the pan together with the sherry, soy sauce, vinegar and sugar. Bring to the boil and simmer for 15 minutes. Take off the heat. Stir in half the coriander. Check the seasoning. Serve, garnishing each bowl with a generous sprinkle of coriander.

NORI SAUSAGES WITH PEPPERONATA AND ARAME

We once served these at an April Fools day menu with celeriac and potato mash, simply billed as sausages and mash. Whether you wish to be as confusing as that is up to you, but unless you are feeding them to brave people, don't tell them that you are actually feeding them two kinds of seaweed.

Toasted sushi nori is a beautiful dark green colour. If you can only get hold of the untoasted variety you have to grill it yourself. The easiest way to do this is to hold it briefly over an open flame (about 5 seconds either side) until it changes colour and crinkles.

Although the method of preparation is a little similar to sushi, some of the ingredients and the method of serving would horrify a Japanese chef. However, since I demonstrated how to cook Place Below-style tofu on Japanese TV and the Japanese makers of the programme said they liked it even though it was deeply untraditional, I've decided to feel comfortable putting deliciousness ahead of tradition.

SERVES 6

SAUSAGES

400 g (14 oz) firm tofu, diced to the size of green peas

MARINADE

100 ml (4 fl oz) red wine
3 tbsp dark soy sauce
3 tbsp water

2 tbsp sesame oil
1 tbsp Tabasco

400 ml (14 fl oz) basmati rice
1 inch ginger

1 bulb garlic
2 tbsp rice wine vinegar (not rice vinegar which is much harsher)
1 tbsp honey (or sugar if you are making this for a vegan)

a little wasabi powder (or 1 tsp hot English mustard)
2 tbsp dark soy sauce
12 sheets toasted sushi nori

1. Marinate the tofu overnight (alternatively, leave out the water in the marinade and marinate it for just a couple of hours). Drain and keep the marinade for re-using, putting in soups etc.

2. Pre-heat the oven to 240°C (475°F/Gas Mark 9). Spread out the tofu on a baking sheet and turn it in the sesame oil and Tabasco. Roast for about 25 minutes until it is going brown and crispy. (The length of time taken will vary greatly depending on whether you are cooking other things in your oven at the same time.)

3. Meanwhile put the rice in a pan with a lid and slightly more than one and a half times its own volume of salted water – about 650 ml (1 pint 3 fl oz). Bring to the boil with the lid off then turn down very low, put the lid on and simmer gently for about 10 minutes. Turn the heat off and leave it to continue to cook in its own steam for another ten minutes or so. Turn out into a large mixing bowl, and mix with the roasted tofu. Whizz the garlic and ginger with the rice wine vinegar and honey and mix well with the rice and tofu mix. Taste and adjust the seasoning (bearing in mind that the nori you are using for 'skin' will be quite salty).

4. To prepare the sausages, mix a little wasabi with half soy sauce and half water to make a thin paste. Lay a sheet of toasted nori on a clean work surface and brush with the soy/wasabi mix. You are then going to proceed as for a jam roly-poly or a spinach roulade. Put a couple of tablespoons of the rice mixture on to the nori making a neat thin oblong with a small gap at the side nearest to you and a gap of about one third of the sheet at the end furthest from you and a gap about a thumb's width on either side of the sheet. Then, starting with the edge nearest to you, slowly and carefully begin to roll the sausage up, keeping the roll as tight as possible. When you have just got the roll started, tuck in the side edges

on top of the rice mixture and continue rolling. The sausage is sealed by the unfilled bit of nori at the far edge. You will find this is all much easier if you don't put too much filling in. Your first sausage will almost certainly be a complete mess (unless you made a lot of *Blue Peter* items as a child) but persevere and after two or three you will be working with the dexterity of a Japanese sushi chef. (Actually, they say it takes 10 years to learn the art of sushi making, so I may be exaggerating slightly.)

You can eat the sausages cold with an oriental salad, but I think they are most delicious hot. To heat them, you really need a microwave – on a fairly high-powered microwave it takes about 30 seconds per sausage, but you should experiment with your machine.

For the pepperonata and arame

4 red peppers, in fat long strips
4 yellow peppers, in fat long strips
3 tbsp olive oil
1 large onion, sliced to half circles
2 cloves garlic, crushed
3 tbsp olive oil
1 tin tomatoes, whizzed
1 packet arame, soaked for about thirty minutes and drained
1 good sized bunch of flat parsley, finely chopped

1. Preheat the oven to 220°C (425°F/Gas Mark 7). Roast the peppers in 3 tablespoons of olive oil until going tender and beginning to colour.

2. Meanwhile make the tomato sauce. Sweat the onion and garlic in the second 3 tablespoons of olive oil until the onions are very tender and sweet. Add the puréed tomatoes and simmer for about 20 minutes.

3. Add the roast peppers, the drained arame and the chopped parsley. Reheat and check the seasoning. Serve warm but not piping hot with the nori sausages.

HAZELNUT MERINGUE CAKE WITH RASPBERRY SAUCE

This is a recipe that came to us from Leith's – a fantastic cookery school which has trained two of the best chefs we've had in the 10 years of our existence.

The season for British raspberries has gradually been extended, not by conning the plants into thinking it's a different time of year, but by developing new varieties, such as Autumn Bliss, which naturally ripen in August/September and even later.

SERVES 8 GENEROUSLY

You need two 19 cm (7½ inch) springform tins

125 g (4 oz) hazelnuts
5 egg whites
Pinch of salt
250 g (8 oz) caster sugar
1 tsp natural vanilla essence
½ tsp white wine vinegar

300 ml (10 fl oz) double cream
1 tbsp caster sugar

300 g (10 oz) raspberries
Juice of half a lemon
50 g (2 oz) icing sugar

1. Toast the hazelnuts. You can either do this in the oven if you have it on anyway, or put them in a dry heavy frying pan and put it on a medium heat, shaking the nuts around from time to time. After about 5 minutes they should be colouring and smelling toasted. Take them off at this point, as they will burn quite quickly. Allow them to cool and then either whizz

them briefly in a food processor, or wrap them in a tea towel and bash vigorously with a rolling pin. You are after a roughly chopped effect, but with some of the hazelnuts a bit more finely ground. You don't want any whole hazelnuts remaining.

2. Line the tins with foil and brush very lightly with a neutral oil such as sunflower oil. Pre-heat the oven to 190°C (375°F/Gas Mark 5).

3. Whisk the egg whites with the pinch of salt until very stiff. If you have a hand-held electric whisk, or a whisk attachment in a Kenwood mixer, these are the easiest tools to use. Add the sugar in a steady stream while continuing to whisk. While still whisking add the vanilla essence and vinegar.

4. Fold the chopped toasted hazelnuts into the egg mixture.

5. Divide between the two lined cake tins and spread carefully into the edges. Bake in the pre-heated oven for about 40 minutes, until the meringue is well set. Allow to cool on wire racks. You may well find that it sinks in the middle. This is fine and you will fill the dip with cream.

6. Whip together the double cream and tablespoon of caster sugar until the cream holds its shape. Fill one of the meringues with cream and then place the second one wrong way up on top of it.

7. Make the sauce. Warm the raspberries, the icing sugar and lemon juice very slightly in a pan so that the icing sugar dissolves. You can then either simply whizz it in a blender and serve it as it is, or pass it through a sieve if you don't like raspberry pips getting in the gaps between your teeth. Before serving check the sauce for sweetness and adjust with icing sugar and lemon juice.

8. Pour the sauce on to each slice of cake when it is cut – it will look very messy if you pour it over the whole cake.

Harvest supper 2: simple and delicious

CORN ON THE COB

If you want to serve a starter with this supper, how about corn on the cob with melted butter? For some reason this seems to have gone out of fashion, despite the fact that it is cheap, easy and quick to cook, and a pleasure to eat so long as you have somebody present who will lick the butter off your chin for you. At any rate, September is the time to eat it. Peel off the leaves and hairy bits and boil in a large pan of water for about 10 minutes. You don't need the special forks to poke in each end – ordinary forks or asbestos fingers will do fine.

There was a marvellous bit in Sophie Grigson's *Eat Your Greens* when she dined with an organic sweetcorn enthusiast. He insisted that the sweetness of the corn decreased with every second after you picked it, so they were filmed doing a frenetic dash from vegetable patch to kitchen and then drooling excitedly over the sweetest corn ever tasted. I haven't had the chance to repeat this experiment, but so long as the cob feels firm and looks unblemished when you have stripped it, it should taste great.

RATATOUILLE WITH ASIAN FLAVOURS AND ROAST TOFU

✶

I think that my favourite recipe from the first Place Below cookery book was the ratatouille, developed in an early 90s flush of vegetable roasting and extra virgin olive oil. We still make it very often, both in London and Hereford, serving it with pesto mash, bulghur and spiced chickpeas, or a basil and cashew blob.

Here is an East-meets-West variation, perfect for a one-world harvest festival – or just for eating any time. For the Roast Tofu, see page 249.

SERVES 6

700 g (1 lb 9 oz) aubergine, diced fairly small
2 red peppers, in fat strips
2 yellow peppers, in fat strips
450 g (1 lb) courgettes, thick slices cut on the bias
200 ml (7 fl oz) olive oil

250 g (8 oz) onions, halved and sliced
3 tbsp olive oil
3 cloves garlic, crushed or finely chopped
15 g (½ oz) ginger root (a 2 cm/1 inch piece), finely chopped
2 tsp lemon grass purée (or one stick of lemon grass very finely chopped)
2 tsp turmeric
½ tsp chilli powder
Salt and freshly ground black pepper

400 g (14 oz) tin plum tomatoes, whizzed
400 ml (14 fl oz) tin coconut milk

1 bunch coriander, picked and roughly chopped

1. Pre-heat the oven to 230°C (450°F/Gas Mark 8).

2. First prepare the vegetables and get them roasting. You will need three baking sheets for roasting the three different vegetables. With each of the vegetables to be roasted, place the vegetable in a large mixing bowl and toss it with enough of the first lot of olive oil to coat the pieces without them becoming sodden. You will find that you use about two thirds of the oil on the aubergine and the remaining one third divided equally between the peppers and the courgettes. Season well and toss again. Lay out on the baking sheet in a single layer and place in the oven. The aubergines take longest to cook – about 30 minutes – and err on the side of overcooking them, as underdone aubergines are horrible. The flesh should be turning gold and they should have shrunk somewhat in size. The peppers take about 20 minutes and the courgettes 10 minutes – but you must do it by eye, not stopwatch, as the timing for roasting will be greatly affected by the power of your oven and how full it is relative to its size. The peppers should be soft and beginning to darken at the edges, and the courgettes should still be firm but just beginning to change colour on the cut surface.

3. While the vegetables are roasting, make the sauce. Sweat the onions in the olive oil. After a couple of minutes add the garlic, ginger, lemon grass, turmeric and chilli powder and a generous sprinkle of salt. Continue cooking, stirring very regularly, until the onions are very soft.

4. Add the whizzed tomatoes, bring to the boil and simmer for about 10 minutes, stirring occasionally. Turn the heat down and add the coconut milk. Bring slowly back almost to boiling point and turn off the heat. Stir in the roast vegetables and check the seasoning.

5. When you serve the dish, top each portion with a generous serving of fresh coriander – if you stir it in, it loses its aroma very quickly.

IAN'S SPICED CHICKPEAS

These dry-spiced chickpeas, first cooked for us by Ian Burleigh (manager of The Place Below), are an excellent and simple accompaniment to either occidental or oriental versions of ratatouille.

SERVES 6 AS AN ACCOMPANIMENT

200 g (7 oz) chickpeas, soaked overnight in heavily salted water
3 tbsp olive oil
Salt and pepper
2 tbsp coriander seeds
1 tbsp cumin seeds
1 tbsp paprika

1. Drain the chickpeas and put in a pan with plenty of fresh water. Bring to the boil. Boil fiercely for at least 10 minutes and then simmer for a further hour or so until the chickpeas are thoroughly tender. Drain and set aside. (Chickpea water makes good stock, so hang on to it if you are making any soup.)

2. Meanwhile, toast the cumin and coriander seeds either in the oven or in a dry frying pan until they are just beginning to smell toasted. Then allow to cool and grind in a spice grinder.

While the chickpeas are still warm mix with the olive oil, salt and freshly ground spices and re-heat over a medium heat.

BULGHUR WITH OLIVE OIL AND LIME

450 ml (16 fl oz) water
225 g (8 oz) medium bulghur

3 tbsp olive oil
Juice and zest of half a lime
1 bunch flat parsley, finely chopped
Salt and freshly ground black pepper

1. Bring water to the boil and add a teaspoon of salt.

2. Add the bulghur and bring back to the boil. Turn down the heat and simmer with the lid on until all the water is absorbed and bulghur is tender (3-10 minutes depending on the bulghur).

3. Stir in the olive oil, bulghur, lime juice and chopped parsley. Check the seasoning and serve.

BLACKBERRY AND APPLE CRUMBLE

This must be the classic British autumn pudding recipe. I won't repeat the wonderful Place Below Pear and Apple Crumble recipe from *Food from The Place Below*, but look it up and simply follow that recipe substituting 500 g (1 lb) of blackberries for the pears. Serve with clotted cream or custard.

Seasonal pleasure: autumn fruits

There are so many delicious things ripening in August/September that I want to eat nothing but fruit (well, almost) for a couple of months.

BLACKBERRIES AND AUTUMN RASPBERRIES

Both wild and cultivated blackberries are easily available this month. I would like to say that wild ones are infinitely superior, but I'm not sure. Autumn raspberries are becoming widely available, especially at PYOs. With both kinds of berry make crumbles, jams and late summer puddings (*variations on the Plum and Fig Pudding given on page 196*).

Raspberry and apple cake

19 cm (7 ½ inch) springform cake tin lined with silicone paper

175 g (6 oz) butter, softened
125 g (4 oz) caster sugar
3 eggs
1 tsp almond essence

300 g (10 oz) plain white flour
1 tsp salt
1 tsp cinnamon
1 tsp baking powder
1 tsp bicarbonate of soda

100 ml (3 fl oz) milk
100 ml (3 fl oz) crème fraîche or sour cream

250 g (8 oz) autumn raspberries
250 g (8 oz) eating apples e.g. Cox's or Russets,
cored and chopped into raspberry-sized pieces

1. Pre-heat the oven to 180°C (350°F/Gas Mark 4).

2. Cream butter and sugar. Beat in eggs slowly.

3. Mix flour, salt, cinnamon, baking powder and bicarbonate of soda.

4. Mix milk and crème fraîche (or sour cream, whichever you're using) together.

5. Alternately mix the dry ingredients and the milk/crème fraîche mixtures into the egg/sugar/butter, bit by bit, beginning and ending with the dry ingredients.

6. Fold the apples and raspberries into the cake mix.

7. Bake for about an hour until a cocktail stick inserted in the centre comes out clean.

8. Dust with icing sugar and serve warmish with crème fraîche or clotted cream.

GRAPES

The European grape harvest is at its height in September. I particularly look out for the fat Italian Muscat grapes. Seedless grapes are available all year round, but this is the time of year when you are likely to find the most tasty ones. My American step-grandmother used to feed us a wonderful dish of seedless grapes tossed in sour cream (crème fraîche would do fine), topped with dark brown sugar and then briefly put under the grill.

PLUMS

Greengages and other green and yellow plums start in August and continue into September and are certainly the best plums both for eating and cooking. We make sauces for cheesecakes, (cook them with sugar and a drop of water and then pass through a sieve), fools (fold greengage purée into whipped cream), greengage sauce, jams (*see August recipe on page 164*) and ice cream (*use the recipe for Bridget's Strawberry Ice Cream on page 145*); and see the Poached Pear recipe on page 239 for a way of poaching plums in red wine. For an even more intense flavour use damsons (in season during September) for any of these things. I think damsons are wonderful but some people find their flavour too strong.

All plums have an acidity which works well with fatty, savoury foods. The next recipe is a good example and one which we use a lot in sandwiches at this time of year.

Warm Brie on toast with plum compote
(or warm Brie and plum sandwich)

I think that the deep-fried Brie with sweet muck on the side that is a standard in freezer-filled pub menus is revolting.

This, however, is mouth-wateringly rich and wonderful. Good bread, good Brie, fruity accompaniment – and don't leave the Brie in the oven too long. For an even more luxurious version use Vacherin, a rare example of a genuinely seasonal cheese. It has a fantastic farmyard smell and is made only from the milk of specific breeds of cattle once they have been brought in from the outside pasture and are fed on silage. It is only available during the winter months.

We started serving this as a hot sandwich in our first winter at the Café in Hereford. Initially we used damson cheese (a very well set, sweetened damson purée) but we have also used damson jam and more recently, I've started doing the same but with a rough, slightly less sweet, jammy compote. If you want to serve it as a toasted sandwich, just put more buttered bread in the oven to toast, and cut the Brie more thinly.

The recipe makes more plum compote than you need, so eat the rest with yoghurt or on croissants.

(You can do the cooking under the grill, but it neither toasts so effectively, nor melts so evenly.)

SERVES 6 AS A STARTER

500 g (1 lb) plums (e.g. Marjorie's seedlings or Victoria's)
100 g (4 oz) caster sugar
4 slices of olive oil bread (either home-made from page 133 or
shop-bought foccacia or other white or whitish country bread)
Butter for spreading
300 g (10 oz) Brie de Meaux, or other good smelly farmhouse Brie
Watercress or rocket to garnish if you like

1. Halve the plums and put in a lidded pan with a splash of water. Cook gently until they are quite collapsed. Take the stones out (it's a bit easier at this point and they probably add a bit of flavour) and add the sugar; bring back to the boil. Simmer vigorously, uncovered, for about 5 minutes and then leave to cool.

2. Pre-heat the oven to 230°C (450°F/Gas Mark 8).

3. Butter the bread and put on a baking sheet in the oven for about 10 minutes until it is crisp and just beginning to colour.

4. Remove from the oven and spread each piece with a dessertspoonful of the plum compote and top with a good slice of Brie, cut roughly to match the shape of the bread. Put back in the oven for about 2 minutes. The Brie should be just beginning to melt and definitely not bubbling.

5. Serve at once, garnished with a little rocket or watercress if you like.

OCTOBER

The season for serious eating begins again – it's getting cold
and we need those calories to protect ourselves

Autumn dinner

Truffled cappuccino of haricot beans and garlic

Butternut squash with ricotta and thyme pesto stuffing
with a salad of baby gem, waxy potatoes, beef tomatoes and
avocado with a saffron dressing

Autumn pudding with plums and fresh figs

Autumn supper

Beetroot, potato and goat's cheese gratin with broccoli,
olive oil and lime

Pear, chocolate and crème fraîche tart
(or roast pears with chocolate sauce)

Seasonal obsession: wild mushrooms

Everything you wanted to know about cepes but were afraid to ask

Autumn dinner

TRUFFLED CAPPUCCINO OF HARICOT BEANS AND GARLIC

I made this after having a really amazing soup based on similar ingredients at Gordon Ramsay's *Aubergine* restaurant in London (since moved to the former *Tante Claire* premises in Royal Hospital Road, Chelsea). I have a suspicion that mine is a simpler version ... this is a wonderful soup both with and without the grated truffle on top, so don't think it's not worth bothering with just because you don't fancy splashing out on fresh truffles although why people want to spend their money on new cars when they could be buying truffles, I don't know. If you want some truffle flavour but don't want a new mortgage, add a little truffle oil just before you froth the soup. You can also add a tiny squiggly drizzle as a garnish to each cup.

Gordon Ramsay's version comes with sautéed girolles (wild mushrooms) in the bottom of the cup. This is delicious. Also good, and easier to get hold of, are oyster mushrooms. Again, if you are having mushrooms elsewhere in the meal, then don't put them in here – the soup on its own, with or without truffles and mushrooms, is something special.

It might seem gimmicky frothing the soup up like a cappuccino, but it really adds something to the pleasure of eating this creamy concoction – especially if, in the place of chocolate on your cappuccino, you find grated truffle on your soup.

The quantity of garlic is not a mistake. The flavour of simmered garlic is many times milder than raw or fried garlic.

In most cases I feel that life is too short to pass puréed soups through a sieve, but here you want something really fine and delicate and it is worth the extra trouble.

See the recipe on page 130 for a note about truffle oil.

100 g (4 oz) haricot beans, soaked overnight in plenty of water

125 g (4 oz) oyster mushrooms
250 g (8 oz) garlic (5 small/medium heads)
1 litre (1¾ pints) whole milk
2 bay leaves
2 cloves
25 g (1 oz) butter

2 tbsp sunflower oil
250 g (8 oz) oyster mushrooms (or girolles if you can get hold of them)

A knob of cold butter
A little truffle oil

1. Drain the soaking water from the haricot beans. Put the beans in a pan with a litre of fresh water. Bring to the boil and boil fiercely for 10 minutes with the lid off. Turn the heat down and simmer for well over an hour until the haricot beans are very tender.

2. Meanwhile, bring another pan of water to the boil. When it is boiling, drop the unpeeled cloves of garlic in and boil for 2 minutes. Drain and put the garlic immediately into a bowl of cold water. Leave to cool off for a few minutes then drain and peel the garlic. You should find that the skins come off quite easily at this point.

3. If you are using oyster mushrooms (see note in the introduction) sweat the first batch in the butter in a large pan until soft. Add the peeled garlic, milk, bay leaves and cloves. Bring to the boil and simmer for 30 minutes. Whizz with a stick blender or in a food processor and pass through a fine sieve. Check the seasoning.

4. If using mushrooms, fry the rest of the oyster mushrooms in small batches until each mushroom is browned on both sides and well seasoned. Put aside to keep warm.

5. You must have warm bowls for this soup. And to follow the joke through, they should really be great big warmed cappuccino cups.

6. Don't do the final preparation for this soup until you are sure that everyone is ready to eat. When you are ready to serve the soup, divide the sautéed oyster mushrooms between the warmed cups. Add the cold butter and truffle oil to the soup. With a stick blender froth up the soup. Basically you just whizz it as normal, but carefully lifting the blender towards the surface of the soup (being careful not to spray the room with it) so that it incorporates some extra air. When you have a layer of froth on top, ladle this in to the first cup with a bit of the liquid from underneath. You want the bowl to be half froth, half liquid. You probably need to re-whizz the soup every one or two servings to get a bit of extra froth. Finally (if you have managed to get hold of any) grate a little truffle onto each bowl and serve and eat at once.

BUTTERNUT SQUASH WITH RICOTTA AND THYME PESTO STUFFING WITH A SALAD OF BABY GEM, WAXY POTATOES, BEEF TOMATOES AND AVOCADO WITH A SAFFRON DRESSING

The classic herb to combine with pumpkin or squash is sage, but fresh thyme is also a good partner. If you have fresh rosemary but not thyme, that is also good in this dish. Don't use both herbs together and certainly do not substitute dried thyme, which is a fairly pointless commodity.

Either curly or flat leaf parsley is fine, but curly parsley is currently easier and cheaper to buy in sensible quantities.

The stuffed squash can be made completely the day before, and simply put in the oven 30–40 minutes before you want to eat. Remember that the squash takes around an hour and a half to bake before you stuff it, so allow yourself enough time. I haven't tried this recipe with gem squash, which seems to be increasingly available in the autumn, but I suspect it would be very good.

SERVES 4

Stuffed squash

1 medium/large butternut squash (about 750 g /1½ lb)
25 g (1 oz) parsley
250 g (8 oz) ricotta
80 g (3 oz) freshly grated Parmesan
2 good sprigs of thyme stripped from the stalk (or a good sprig of rosemary,
the leaves stripped from the stalk and finely chopped)
Salt and freshly ground pepper

1. Pre-heat the oven to 200°C (400°F/Gas Mark 6).

2. Wrap the squash in foil and put on a baking dish in the oven for about 1½ hours or until it is very soft. It is very difficult to overcook the squash at this stage, so if you are uncertain if it is cooked enough leave it in a little bit longer. Take out and allow to cool.

3. The squash will now be quite floppy, so handle it carefully so that it more or less retains its shape. Cut the squash in half lengthways and scoop out the seeds and any fibrous flesh surrounding them and discard. Then, using a dessert spoon, carefully scoop out the flesh, trying to leave the skin intact. (If you do puncture the skin, don't worry; the filling is fairly firm and should not leak out too much.)

4. Mash the squash flesh and mix with the other ingredients except about 30 g (1 oz) (just under half) of the Parmesan. Season to taste with salt and freshly ground black pepper.

5. Divide the filling between the squash shells and smooth off the tops. Pack the stuffed squashes into a small baking dish so that they are supported on all sides and put back in the oven for about 30–40 minutes until they are golden on top. Each half serves two people. (If you found very small butternuts, you could use two for this recipe and give each person half a squash, but you can't normally find them that small.)

Salad of baby gem, waxy potatoes, beef tomatoes and avocado with a saffron dressing

This salad makes a lovely accompaniment to the butternut squash.

550 g (1 lb 4 oz) waxy potatoes (e.g. Charlottes), peeled
1 tbsp white wine vinegar
4 tbsp olive oil
Salt and freshly ground black pepper

80 ml (3 fl oz) white wine
130 mg saffron powder
(one of the tiny packets of powdered saffron) or a pinch of saffron strands
120 ml (4 fl oz) double cream

2 baby gem lettuces
250 g (8 oz) beef tomatoes
1 ripe avocado

1. Put the potatoes in a pan with plenty of water. Bring to the boil and simmer until tender (about 15 minutes). Drain and toss with the vinegar and olive oil. Season with salt and freshly ground black pepper.

2. Put the wine and saffron into a small pan and bring to the boil. Boil fiercely with the lid off to reduce to ⅓ of its original volume. Add the double cream. Bubble for a minute until it thickens and take off the heat. Season and taste. This can be done in advance and the sauce re-heated to blood heat before serving.

3. Arrange the baby gem around the outside of the plates on which the squash will be served. Distribute the potatoes around the lettuce in a random way. On top of that arrange the tomato, cut into thin slices. At the last minute peel the avocado and cut into thin slices and arrange on top. Dribble the warmed saffron sauce around the salad and plonk the stuffed butternut in the middle of the plate. Picasso had nothing on this.

AUTUMN PUDDING WITH PLUMS AND FRESH FIGS

One of the great things about moving to Hereford is that the Walnut Tree Inn is very much closer than it is to Twickenham. Last year I had an autumn pudding there, made in the same way as summer pudding but with a mixture of dried fruit. We have tried several variations on this theme. The main thing is that the fruit must be soft (e.g. pears can only be used very sparingly) and must produce a lot of juice. The current favourite at The Place Below features cranberries, plums and blackberries, but this recipe is for a luxurious alternative with only plums and fresh figs.

The first time I made this at home I bought some fantastic organic Lebanese figs from the brilliant greengrocer at the top of our road (Freshers in East Twickenham). My wife subsequently blamed the figs (which are apparently grown in a small gap between the Syrian army, the Israeli army and a PLO camp) for the onset of labour – our son Jonathan arrived the next morning.

Serve with either clotted cream or crème fraîche.

SERVES 8

1 kg (2 lb) dark plums (e.g. President), halved and stoned
200 g (7 oz) caster sugar
1 kg (2 lb) fresh ripe figs, cut in quarters and with the hard bobble removed
1 large loaf thick sliced white bread

1. Put the plums in a lidded pan with a tiny splash of water (if you've washed them just before, the residue from the washing will be sufficient). Put on a low heat with the lid on, stirring regularly. You can turn the heat up a bit as the juice begins to run. Continue cooking until the plums are mushy – if they are very ripe this will not take more than a few minutes. Add the sugar and stir it in until it has completely dissolved. Take the plums off the heat. Stir in the chopped figs.

2. Put a large bowl under a colander and drain the fruit mixture thoroughly. Retain the juice.

3. Cut the crusts off the bread. Line a large mixing bowl with the bread, soaking each piece thoroughly but quickly in the fruit syrup before putting it into the bowl. This is a bit like building a wall. As you go up the sides of the bowl you need to cut the bits of bread into shapes to create a complete patchwork up the sides of the bowl with neither holes nor overlaps and leaving a reasonably even rim at the top. You should use about two-thirds of the bread on the base and sides of the bowl. Pour the drained fruit into the lined bowl and top it with the rest of the soaked bread. Put a plate on top which is smaller than the top of the bowl, weight it down with more plates or a heavy tin, and then put it in the fridge overnight on a deep tray to catch any juice which spills down the sides. If you have any juice left over from the construction, keep it to use either as a sauce or, diluted with fizzy mineral water, a delicious drink.

4. The next day turn the pudding out onto a large flat plate with a rim, cut carefully with a serrated knife and serve with clotted cream or crème fraîche.

Autumn supper

BEETROOT, POTATO AND GOAT'S CHEESE GRATIN WITH BROCCOLI, OLIVE OIL AND LIME

Goat's cheese goes well with all things sweet – in salads with roast sweet potatoes, in tarts with roasted sweet peppers, and in gratins with baked beetroot.

The season for domestically grown beetroot should be in full swing by now. If you have bought your beetroots (or indeed dug them from your own vegetable patch) with their tops still on and in good condition, then instead of the broccoli accompaniment you could serve them with beet tops, chopped, boiled for about 10 minutes (they are tougher than spinach and need more vigorous treatment), then drained and tossed in melted butter and a dollop of hot English mustard.

800 g (1 lb 12 oz) beetroot, raw

1 kg (2 lb 4 oz) potatoes

250 ml (9 fl oz) double cream

75 g (3 oz) mature goat's cheese

50 g (2 oz) mature Cheddar, grated

1 clove garlic, crushed

Scrape of nutmeg

Salt and freshly ground black pepper

75 g (3 oz) breadcrumbs

1. Bake the beetroots the day before. (Put in deep metal trays and cover them with foil then put in a hot oven for about 1½ hours. Check that they are tender and then leave to cool overnight.)

2. Peel and slice the beetroot about 1 cm (½ inch) thick.

3. Slice the potatoes about 1 cm (½ inch) thick and boil in salted water until not quite cooked.

4. Mix the beetroot, potato, cream, goat's cheese, half the grated Cheddar, the garlic, nutmeg, salt and freshly ground pepper in a large bowl (more than one if necessary, depending on the quantities).

5. Put into a large baking dish. Mix the remaining grated Cheddar with the breadcrumbs and scatter on top of the bakes.

6. Serve with either Savoy cabbage or broccoli, blanched and tossed in olive oil and a little lime juice (see below).

Broccoli with olive oil and lime

800 g (1 lb 12 oz) broccoli, in florets,
with the tender part of the stalk sliced thinly and diagonally
4 tbsp olive oil
Juice and zest of a lime
Salt and freshly ground black pepper

1. Bring a large pan of water to the boil. Just before you are ready to eat put the broccoli in. Bring it back to the boil and as soon as the broccoli is tender (this will only be a minute or two) drain it thoroughly.

2. Mix with the olive oil, lime juice and zest and season to taste with salt and freshly ground black pepper. Serve at once.

PEAR, CHOCOLATE AND CRÈME FRAÎCHE TART (OR ROAST PEARS WITH CHOCOLATE SAUCE)

You can either serve this as a chilled tart or serve the roast pears hot from the oven with the chocolate and crème fraîche mixture served warm as a sauce. Either way, it is a chocolate lover's dream.

4 small pears, not too ripe
25 g (1 oz) butter
25 g (1 oz) molasses sugar

1 x 23 cm (9 inch) sweet pastry tart case, baked blind (see page x)

2 dsp jelly type jam — elderberry is particularly good, redcurrant would also be fine

150 g (6 oz) dark chocolate
200 ml (7 fl oz) crème fraîche

1. Pre-heat the oven to 220°C (425°F/Gas Mark 7).

2. Quarter the pears and core them. Then melt the butter and stir in the sugar. If you are using molasses sugar, or another dark brown sugar then you need to be sure to break up the large lumps or they will tend to burn. Toss the pear quarters in the melted butter and sugar and spread them out on a small baking sheet. Place in the pre-heated oven. Turn the pears over and baste them after about 5 minutes. After a further 5 minutes they should be quite tender and the butter/sugar mixture should be beginning to caramelise. Take them out of the oven and set aside to cool.

3. Brush the base and sides of the blind baked tart case with the jelly. Depending how solid the jelly, is you may need to warm it slightly to make this easy. Then arrange the pears on the jellied case.

4. Break the chocolate into chunks and put in a heavy-bottomed pan with crème fraîche. Put on a low heat and stir regularly until the chocolate has nearly all melted. Take it off the heat at this stage and keep stirring to finish off the melting.

5. Pour the chocolate mixture evenly over the pears in the tart case and put the whole thing in the fridge to chill for a couple of hours or until the chocolate has set.

If you want to serve this as roast pears with a chocolate sauce, simply time the pear roasting to be ready when you are ready for pudding and warm up the sauce just prior to serving. Served this way, you might want to have a bit of extra crème fraîche to serve with it.

Seasonal obsession: wild mushrooms

I have had a phase of being seriously obsessed by wild mushrooms. Villa holidays in Italy would be dominated by trips to the clammiest woods where I was hopeful of the most interesting finds; we would be having a perfectly normal swimming pool and eating holiday in France and I would insist on searching out the local professor of mycology who proceeded to abuse us for wanting to eat what for him were simply scientific specimens; we would regularly dirty the counter of pristine French pharmacies with piles of confusing looking fungi which the pharmacist would proceed to divide expertly between 'comestible', 'toxique' and, the most exciting-sounding, 'toxique mortelle'.

Walks around where we live in Hereford would be dominated for part of the year by constant bending for field mushrooms, parasols and puffballs. One batch of parasols we fried and finished with some Chateau Musar (Lebanese red wine) and cream. The next day we were going to eat at the Walnut Tree Inn, and found some more parasols on our appetite-building pre-prandial walk up the Skirrid. I proudly offered them at the bar, only to be told that parasols and alcohol produce a severe allergic reaction in many people and they were certainly not interested in cooking with them!

At last, I think I am now in what is technically known as 'recovery'. The number of genuinely delicious wild mushrooms which I have found on these numerous expeditions has been rather small. However, from regular purchases from the wonderful Tony Booth (*see page* 3) I am clearer about which varieties of wild mushrooms are really special – and for those I am currently a purchaser not a forager.

Morels are probably my absolute favourite, and are the one variety whose European season is in the spring not the autumn (*see page* 102). Next in my order of preference come cepes (porcini in Italian, penny buns in English), which I heretically think are much more interesting dried than fresh. I have eaten fresh cepes cooked by me and by lots of French chefs and I have only once had ones which are anything other than unattractively slimy. During a memorable meal at Restaurant Michel Bras outside Laguiole we ate small cepes (which are even more difficult to get hold of than large ones) which had been fried on a very high heat and were delicious. Dried cepes, however, are always a fantastic thing. Their aroma as they re-hydrate is for me up there with baking bread and grinding coffee as one of the great kitchen smells – but it's a love it or hate it smell, and I know lots of people who find it quite repulsive. The liquor produced by the re-hydration is wonderful for soups (*see page 170*), sauces (*see page 235*) and risottos (*see page 5*). Dried cepes are now easy to find in supermarkets or delicatessens.

The other two woodland mushrooms with which I have had real success are pieds de mouton (hedgehog mushrooms) and girolles. Both are delicious fried with pasta or in a Mushroom Tart (*see page 232*), and girolles make a wonderful addition to the Haricot Bean Soup on page 25.

Despite their wonderful name, trompettes de mort ('trumpets of death') are ultra fiddly to clean and not very exciting in flavour. Cepes are a variety of boletus mushroom; most of the other members of the family, which often make up a large part of what is sold as 'melange de foret' (mixed woodland mushrooms), are not especially nice.

Of the mushrooms commonly found in fields, field mushrooms and horse mushrooms can be excellent, but some varieties seem to have a uric smell, which I find quite off-putting. I would like to prefer wild ones but actually I prefer commercially grown field mushrooms. I think parasol mushrooms are very tasty – but see the Walnut Tree warning above. Giant puffballs, which I was very excited by the sight of, I think are rather uninteresting, although not unpleasant, to eat.

In all of this, be careful. Don't eat mushrooms unless you are sure of the variety – to the non-expert like me, it is easy to get confused between the toxic and the edible varieties. If you are unsure, get advice from someone more experienced before eating.

Some mushrooms which are more recently domesticated, and therefore much cheaper to buy, are oyster mushrooms, shitake and pied bleu. All of these are very tasty but should not be described as wild mushrooms.

NOVEMBER

At The Place Below we've found November is often a
peak month for pleasure dinners – before duty entertaining
gets under way in December.

All Saints' dinner

Pumpkin, sage and lentil soup

Field mushrooms stuffed with roast tofu and shallots,
with cepe gravy, parsnip and potato mash and Savoy cabbage
in a balsamic cream

Fig and banana tarte tatin

Winter supper dishes

Pumpkin and sage risotto

Leek and Caerphilly potato cakes

Beetroot and red onion ragout

Mushroom, Stilton and pumpkin pie with lime pickle roast potatoes

Seasonal pleasure

British fruit with British cheeses

All Saints' dinner

PUMPKIN, SAGE AND LENTIL SOUP

I suggest you use the slightly larger size of pumpkin (of the two given below), but don't use the huge pumpkins offered for decorations at Hallowe'en time. They tend to be watery and tasteless. Bake all of it and then use the remainder of the baked pumpkin for risotto, or a dip, mixed with cream cheese and Parmesan. It's probably easiest to bake the pumpkin the day before. Although it takes a long time in the oven, you don't have to do anything to it while it's in there.

Adding some extra olive oil when the soup is being puréed adds extra richness and a different flavour and texture, as against simply adding more olive oil at the beginning of the cooking process. This seems to work particularly well with soups based on pulses.

1 very small pumpkin (about 750 g/1½ lb) or half a larger one

1 medium leek (about 200 g/7 oz), sliced and washed
4 tbsp olive oil
2 good sized cloves garlic, crushed
10 large sage leaves, finely chopped

125 g (4 oz) red lentils
1.5 litres (2¾ pints) water

5 more sage leaves, finely chopped
2 tbsp olive oil
Juice of ½ a lemon
Salt and freshly ground black pepper

1. Pre-heat the oven to 230°C (450°F/Gas Mark 8).

2. Wrap the pumpkin in foil and place on a baking sheet in the oven. Bake for 1½–2 hours until it feels very tender when you prod it or insert a knife. Set aside to cool. When it is cool, cut in half and scoop out the seeds, then peel and cut into large chunks. (Put any you don't need for the soup under clingfilm or in a closed plastic box in the fridge.)

3. In a large pan sweat the leeks, garlic and first batch of sage leaves in the first lot of olive oil until the leeks are soft, adding a little salt after the first couple of minutes.

4. Add the water and lentils and bring to the boil. Simmer for about 25 minutes, or until the lentils are quite mushy. Add the cubed, baked pumpkin and bring back to the boil.

5. Take off the heat and add the second lot of sage leaves and olive oil and the lemon juice and blend very thoroughly. Season generously with salt and pepper – both lentils and pumpkin require generous seasoning – and serve. For fancier presentation, garnish with fresh sage leaves.

FIELD MUSHROOMS STUFFED WITH ROAST TOFU AND SHALLOTS, WITH CEPE GRAVY, PARSNIP AND POTATO MASH AND SAVOY CABBAGE WITH BALSAMIC CREAM

This is another great winter gravy-and-mash combination which dates from the early days of The Place Below. It is also the only recipe I have demonstrated on Japanese TV – the Japanese presenter found this highly inauthentic (but in my view very delicious) way of cooking tofu rather amusing. I felt at a considerable disadvantage since he was talking to the camera in Japanese, laughing merrily and pointing at my food, and I was standing there trying to look haughty and chef-like – not a pose I've ever mastered.

To make the parsnip and potato mash, follow the recipe for Celeriac and Potato Mash (*see page* 236), but substituting parsnip for celeriac. The important thing to remember is that you first make a thin buttery purée with the parsnip in a blender and then fold that into the potato which you have mashed with a masher. If you blend everything together it will go gloopy because of the starch from the potato; if on the other hand you try to mash the parsnip, you won't get a smooth purée since it doesn't mash in the same way that potato does.

The recipe for the cepe gravy is given as part of the Christmas dinner on page 235.

If you really like big field mushrooms (I do), then double up on the quantity and put one on top of the stuffing (this one gill-side downwards) as well as the one underneath. If they fall apart too easily, attach them together with a cocktail stick while they are heating in the oven.

150 ml (5 fl oz) dark soy sauce
150 ml (5 fl oz) red wine
2 cloves garlic, crushed
1 cm (½ inch) fresh root ginger, finely chopped

350 g (12 oz) firm tofu
2 tbsp sesame oil
1 tsp Tabasco

225 g (8 oz) shallots, peeled and quartered
2 tbsp olive oil

6 or 12 (see introduction) very large field mushrooms
4 tbsp olive oil
2 cloves garlic, crushed
Pinch chilli powder
Salt and pepper

1. Prepare the stuffing first. Mix together the marinade ingredients (soy sauce, red wine, garlic and ginger). Cut the tofu into 32 small cubes, place in a dish and pour the marinade over it. Leave in the fridge for a couple of hours. (If you are leaving it to marinate overnight, add some water to the marinade or the tofu will end up too salty.)

2. Preheat the oven to 220°C (425°F/Gas Mark 7). Drain off the marinade and set it aside for the Cepe Gravy (*see page 235*). Gently turn the tofu cubes in the sesame oil and Tabasco, season and arrange with the shallots on a baking sheet. Roast for about 30 minutes or until the tofu is just crisp on the outside and the shallots are tender but not squashy.

3. You don't need to peel the mushrooms. Put the olive oil, garlic, chilli and seasoning in a blender and process until combined. Brush the mushrooms with the oil and garlic mixture, place on an oiled baking sheet and bake until the mushrooms are just beginning to give out their juices.

4. Transfer the mushrooms to a baking dish and divide the roast shallot and tofu stuffing equally between them. There should be a little mountain of stuffing in each one. (If you are using double mushroom quantities, put the second one on top of each stuffed mushroom at this point.) Return to the oven for 20 minutes until sizzling hot.

Serve with the Cepe Gravy, Parsnip Mash, and the Cabbage in Balsamic Cream (*see below*).

Savoy cabbage with balsamic cream

There is a delicious recipe in *Food from The Place Below* for roast aubergines and Puy lentils with balsamic vinegar and cream. This cabbage dish uses the same flavours much more simply.

SERVES 6

1 fairly small Savoy cabbage, finely chopped
2 scant tbsp balsamic vinegar
6 tbsp double cream
Salt and freshly ground black pepper

Bring a large pan of water to the boil and add the cabbage. Bring back to the boil and simmer for 1 minute. Drain and return to the pan with the balsamic vinegar and cream. Put back on a medium heat and stir around until the ingredients are well mixed and heated through. Season with salt and freshly ground black pepper and serve.

FIG AND BANANA TARTE TATIN

Figs are readily available from different parts of Europe from September until the end of the year. They are one of the great pleasures of autumn and early winter, but also one of the most variable fruits. A dried up or an unripe fig is not at all interesting, but ripe, sweet, juicy, sticky figs are a real luxury. My best fig memory (apart from the birth of my son – see page 196) is being on holiday with a fig tree (and Sarah) in France in September, and going out each day and gently squeezing the figs to see which were ready to eat. They seemed to ripen at the rate of about ten a day which suited us fine, and they were warm from the sun and exceptionally delicious.

If you get absolutely perfect figs like these (relatively rare in the UK) then just eat them as they are, or with a little runny honey and Greek yoghurt, or cut up in a salad with some new potatoes dressed in olive oil and thyme, some watercress and a little crumbled Roquefort.

But if the figs you buy are a little on the firm side, or in some other way not quite up to scratch, there is nothing better to do with them than bake them with bananas, honey, butter and lemon – or go the whole hog and make this fig and banana tarte tatin.

SERVES 8

Juice of half a lemon
50 g (2 oz) dark brown sugar
50 g (2 oz) butter
450 g (1 lb) bananas (3 medium ones)
6 largish purple figs

400 g (14 oz) puff pastry

1. Pre-heat the oven to 240°C (475°F/Gas Mark 9).

2. Put the butter, lemon juice and sugar in a deep heavy pizza pan or tarte tatin tin. Put on a medium heat and stir together.

3. Take off the heat and slice the bananas (lengthways) and the figs (in quarters) and arrange with the uncut surfaces downwards in the butter mixture. Put back on a medium heat until the mixture begins to bubble. Put in the oven for about 40 minutes until the juice has become quite syrupy.

4. Roll out the pastry and put over the fruit. Bake for about 20 minutes until puffed up and golden. Turn upside-down to serve. Serve with crème fraîche.

Winter supper dishes

PUMPKIN AND SAGE RISOTTO

All the members of the squash family like to be cooked with fresh sage. In this risotto you cook some squash to melt into the rice, and roast some separately to caramelise it and perch on top of the creamy risotto.

The proportion of usable flesh to total weight varies enormously with pumpkins, so in recipes using pumpkins I have used the peeled and de-seeded weight rather than the total vegetable weight as a guide. You will almost always buy more pumpkin than you need for a single recipe anyway, simply because of their size.

The two members of the pumpkin family I have used most successfully for this risotto are the Crown Prince pumpkin (which I have to admit I have only ever seen for sale at our local pick-your-own at Oakchurch in Herefordshire) and gem squash, which is much more widely available. Both have green, tough skins, and the flesh is very firm and a pronounced orange colour. The looser texture and paler colour of the large pumpkins people tend to buy for Hallowe'en are an indication of their poorer cooking qualities, despite their fun appearance.

SERVES 4

50 ml (2 fl oz) olive oil
150 g (5 oz) red onion, small dice
150 g (5 oz) leek, small dice
300 g (10 oz) pumpkin, peeled and cut into small dice
2 cloves garlic, crushed
10 leaves fresh sage, finely chopped

400 ml (14 fl oz) dry white wine

250 g (9 oz) risotto rice

400 g (14 oz) pumpkin, peeled and cut into
long wide thin strips following the shape of the pumpkin
2 tbsp olive oil
10 fresh sage leaves, finely chopped

125 g (5 oz) freshly grated Parmesan (or 50 g (2 oz)
Beenleigh Blue and 75 g (3 oz) freshly grated Parmesan)

1. Pre-heat oven to 230°C (450°F/Gas Mark 8).

2. Put the red onion, leek, pumpkin, garlic and the first 10 sage leaves in 50 ml (2 fl oz) of olive oil in a heavy-bottomed, lidded pan on a high heat with the lid on. Stir every 2–3 minutes for the next 10 minutes by which time the vegetables should be softened.

3. Meanwhile put a kettle on to boil and put the wine in a separate saucepan to heat on a high heat.

4. Toss the large bits of squash in 2 tablespoons of olive oil and the second quantity of sage leaves. Spread them on a large oven sheet (don't let them overlap or they won't cook evenly or quickly enough) and put them in the pre-heated oven.

5. When the kettle has boiled add 450 ml (16 fl oz) boiling water to the heating wine. Turn the wine/water mixture off just as it begins to boil.

6. When the onion and squash mixture has softened keep the heat on high, but with the lid now off add the rice and stir vigorously. Immediately add half the diluted wine and stir well, making sure that none of the rice grains have stuck to the bottom of the pan. Keep cooking on a high heat until it boils, then turn down to medium, stirring vigorously at least once a minute. After it has boiled for 5 minutes add the rest of the diluted wine, still cooking on a high heat. When most of the liquid has been absorbed (about a further 7 minutes) check to see if the rice is cooked. There should still be some resistance in the grain but it should have lost its raw, woody texture. At this stage the risotto should be the consistency

of a sloppy stew or a very thick soup. If the rice is not quite cooked, add a little more boiling water and continue cooking for another couple of minutes. Check that the rice is now cooked.

7. Remove from the heat and stir in the freshly grated Parmesan (or mixture of Parmesan and Beenleigh Blue). Taste it and add more salt or some pepper if you think it needs it.

8. Take the large bits of roasting squash out of the oven. They should be very soft and sweet and coloured at the edges.

9. Divide the risotto between the plates and top each plate with its share of the large pieces of roasted squash.

LEEK AND CAERPHILLY POTATO CAKES

I like potato cakes in all sorts of different ways. In summer, we sometimes make one with samphire and Gruyere and serve it with a sorrel and white wine sauce. Or you can use some celeriac with the potato and combine it with blue cheese (try Harbourne Blue, a lovely goat's cheese from the maker of Beenleigh Blue).

This version is the most comforting and reliable. It really makes a difference if you can get hold of a decent, mature Caerphilly such as Duckett's or Gorwyd. If you haven't tried a proper Caerphilly like this before, it will be a complete revelation. Far from the lean crumbliness of a supermarket Caerphilly, these real cheeses have a proper rind with a soft yellowing edge and a whiter centre. A decent cheese like this also makes excellent cheese on toast, whereas its poor relation does not melt properly. A good Lancashire would work equally well – again, try to buy the cheese from a cheese shop where they look after their cheese, since there is a huge variation in cheese called Lancashire. A medium mature Cheddar would also be fine, but would produce a different and rather sharper flavour.

If you want to make the potato cakes the day before, that's fine, and they also re-fry very well if you don't eat them all at the first sitting.

I think that potato cakes of all kinds are best when eaten with something sharp and wet. At its simplest, that can be Heinz tomato ketchup (inferior brands will not do), but if you've got the time, the beetroot and red onion ragout makes a great accompaniment. Some blanched Savoy cabbage tossed in seasoned olive oil would complete a real feast – in fact that's what we had for my wife's last birthday – and people say that you can't eat well on seasonal winter vegetables.

600 g (1 lb 5 oz) potatoes, peeled (or not peeled if you like bits of skin in
your potato cakes – which I do), and cut into large, even-sized chunks
200 g (7 oz) leek, sliced
50 g (2 oz) butter
Salt and freshly ground pepper

1 bunch spring onions, finely chopped
1 good dsp English mustard
175 g (6 oz) good quality Caerphilly, grated
2 eggs, beaten

100 g (4 oz) breadcrumbs (brown or white are fine, and the more flavoursome
bits the bread has in it, such as sesame or sunflower seeds, the better)
About 15 leaves of fresh rosemary, chopped very fine
1 egg, beaten

Sunflower oil for frying

1. Put the potatoes in a large pan with plenty of salted water. Bring to the
   boil and simmer until the potatoes are well cooked but have not completely collapsed, which will take about 15–20 minutes. Drain in a colander, leaving them to drain as dry as possible.

2. Meanwhile, sweat the leeks in the butter with plenty of salt and pepper
   until the leeks are just tender.

3. Turn the well-drained potatoes out into a large mixing bowl and mash
   with a hand masher. Mix gently with the cooked leeks, the spring onions,
   the mustard, the cheese and the two beaten eggs.

4. Mix the breadcrumbs and the chopped fresh rosemary.

5. Form the potato mixture into even sized balls – you should get eight out
   of this quantity. Dip the potato balls into the egg, and then into the bowl
   with the breadcrumb mix, flattening them slightly as you go. Then leave
   them on a tray until you are ready to fry them.

6. About 15 minutes before you are ready to eat, put 3–4 tablespoons of sunflower oil in a large heavy-bottomed frying pan on to a high heat. When the oil is quite hot (at which point it should sloosh about the pan quite freely and should have become much less viscous than it was when it was cold) put in some of the potato cakes and turn the heat down to low/medium. Don't overcrowd the pan or you won't be able to turn them over easily. In a normal large domestic frying pan you probably won't fit more than four cakes at a time comfortably. So either have two pans on the go at the same time, or do them in two batches keeping the first lot warm in a low oven in the meantime.

7. After 7–10 minutes turn them over. They should be a lovely crisp brown on the cooked side. Cook them for a further 5–8 minutes on the other side and serve straight away.

BEETROOT AND RED ONION RAGOUT

You can make this dish with ready-cooked beetroot, but it's never as good as beetroot which you have baked yourself. I now always bake beetroot from raw. It is as different as can be imagined from that horrible vinegared muck which we used to be given at school and which (judging by supermarket shelves) people still for some reason buy.

It's always easiest to bake the beetroots the day before you want to use them. Then they are cool to peel, and you're not worrying about whether they will be done in time for supper.

Bake more than you need for this recipe and the next day, make a simple gratin with sliced beetroot tossed in some crème fraîche and Parmesan, topped with a little more Parmesan mixed with breadcrumbs. Serve it with some blanched broccoli tossed in a little seasoned olive oil or butter; or with some beet tops with butter and mustard (*see note on page 198*). If you're hungry, boil a few potatoes to have with it.

SERVES 4

500 g (1 lb) raw beetroot

200 g (7 oz) red onion (one medium-sized onion), halved and sliced
2 cloves garlic, crushed
2 blobs stem ginger (from a jar of stem ginger in syrup)
or a broad bean sized knob of fresh root ginger, finely diced
Salt

175 ml (6 oz) red wine
50 ml crème fraîche

1. The day before you want to make this, put the beetroot on a baking tray and cover tightly with foil. Put in a medium oven 190°C (375°F/Gas Mark 5) for 2–3 hours until the beetroot is very tender. (It is not particularly sensitive to the temperature, so if you need the oven at a different temperature for something else, that's fine, but adjust the expected cooking time accordingly). When the beetroot is cooked, allow it to cool, and peel it. If you haven't washed it before baking (and there is no reason why you should), be careful as you peel not to spread dirt onto the beautiful glistening peeled beet.

2. The next day, put the onion in a heavy-bottomed pan with the olive oil, garlic and ginger and cook until the onion is soft, adding some salt part way through the cooking.

3. Add the red wine, bring to the boil and cook with the lid off on a high heat for about 10 minutes to reduce the liquid by about half. Add the crème fraîche, bring back to the boil, and take off the heat. Check the seasoning and serve. If you have any fresh dill or fennel hair, chop it finely and sprinkle on top.

MUSHROOM, STILTON AND PUMPKIN PIE

This is a rich pie, so don't give people enormous helpings. If you are a normal human being and don't make your own puff pastry (I don't), it's also quite a quick dish to put together. Most recently I made this pie with chestnut mushrooms, which keep the pie a pale, creamy colour but have a good flavour, if not quite as hefty as large flat or 'field mushrooms'. As with lots of dishes with mushrooms in, you need quite a big pan to cook it in as the mushrooms are extremely bulky before they cook down. My favourite pumpkin for this is the Crown Prince (*see note on page 213*).

It makes a difference if you use a decent Stilton — and don't chuck away the rind when you cook with Stilton. Even if you don't like the rind raw, it is delicious when cooked.

Serve it with Lime Pickle Roast Potatoes (*see page 223*) and some buttered cabbage — or even brussels sprouts, if you're one of those weird people who like Brussels sprouts.

SERVES 4—6

3 tbsp olive oil
4 large sticks celery, sliced
750 g (1½ lb) chestnut mushrooms, sliced in half if they are large
1 clove garlic, crushed
¼ medium pumpkin (300 g/10 oz peeled), cubed
300 ml (10 fl oz) white wine
200 ml (7 oz) double cream
150 g (5 oz) Stilton

1 ready-rolled puff pastry (about 350 g/12 oz)
1 egg, beaten

1. Pre-heat the oven to 220°C (425°F/Gas Mark 7).

2. Heat the olive oil in a large heavy-bottomed pan. Add the celery and mushrooms and a generous pinch of salt and cook over a fairly high heat, stirring regularly until the mushrooms have softened and cooked down. After the first couple of minutes of cooking, add the garlic and continue to stir regularly. Add the cubed pumpkin and continue to cook for 5–10 minutes until the pumpkin has begun to soften.

3. Add the wine. Turn the heat up high and bubble fiercely with the lid off until the volume of liquid is reduced by half. Add the cream and bring back to the boil, and simmer until the sauce is the consistency of very thick cream. Take off the heat and stir in the crumbled Stilton. Spread this mixture over the bottom of a rectangular pie or lasagne dish, top with the ready-rolled puff pastry and brush the pastry with the beaten egg.

4. Bake in the pre-heated oven for about 25 minutes until the pastry is puffy and golden. Serve at once.

LIME PICKLE ROAST POTATOES

This is a version of a delicious dish we ate at L'Odeon restaurant in London's Regent Street when Bruno Loubet was cooking there. It was curious eating a meal in a room which used to be the British Airways inoculation centre, and which I had last visited 20 years earlier to have a series of unpleasant needles put in my arm before setting off on my travels.

I use Sharwoods lime pickle, but any other good lime pickle will be fine. Bear in mind that you can't use large bits of lime here, as the idea is to coat the potatoes. Choose a pickle which has plenty of goo.

SERVES 6

1.2 kg (2 lb 8 oz) potatoes, peeled and cut into large chunks, about the size of a satsuma
4 tbsp sunflower oil
3 dsps (heaped) of lime pickle
Salt

1. Pre-heat the oven to 230°C (450°F/Gas Mark 8).

2. Bring a large pan of salted water to the boil. Add the potatoes, bring back to the boil and simmer until the potatoes are almost cooked (about 10 minutes). Drain well.

3. Return the potatoes to the pan and turn gently in the oil and pickle and some salt.

4. Spread the potatoes out onto a large baking tray and put in the pre-heated oven for about 30–50 minutes until golden and crisp. Serve at once.

(If you are serving the potatoes with the pie, you can quite happily turn the oven down a bit for the pie; they will just take a little longer to cook.)

Seasonal pleasure: British fruit with British cheeses

Apples and pears are yet more commodities which are now universally available. And because of their easy transportability, there are some genuinely tasty alternative apples around (particularly from New Zealand) at times of the year when the British crops are past their best. But for the greatest variety, and the real aroma of appley freshness, then the autumn and early winter is the time to eat British apples and pears.

While I can't get away from the feeling that there is inevitably something workaday about eating apples – you have to chew hard for one thing – when you come to Comice pears, you move into the realms of real luxury. Other pears can be extremely nice when eaten at their peak (even those sold mysteriously by one supermarket as 'economy pears') but a good ripe Comice is one of the really special fruits of the year. There is no point cooking a ripe Comice; it should be eaten as it is. My father-in-law (Jim of the vegetable plot), who is a major Comice fan, reckons that November is the peak time for perfect Comice eating. They are available well into the New Year, but will have spent longer in a cold store. Buy them when they are still green. They are ready to eat when they have turned speckled yellow. The nearest Jim gets to being a Roman slave is when he takes to peeling and coring ripe Comices and feeding them to us as we sit gooing at our baby or engaged in some other vital activity.

The perfect partner for British apples and pears is good cheese. For a simple lunch, bread, Cheddar and a fresh Cox or Russet is hard to beat. Equally good for this kind of eating are decent Caerphilly, Lancashire and Cheshire. The more juicy sweetness of pears seems to go particularly well with hard sheep's cheeses, such as Tynig or Berkswell (or, if you are feeling less patriotic, pecorino). Good pears and good sheep's cheese make one of my favourite endings for a meal. For something more elaborate, try the Roast Pear and Stilton Sandwich described on page 138.

Cheeses, particularly the majority which require controlled ripening, continue to be something that supermarkets do not do nearly as well as specialist cheese shops. Seek out your local cheese shop and go there regularly. If in West London seek out Vivian's in Richmond; if in Hereford or Leominster, go to Mark Hindle's excellent 'Mousetrap' shops where, alongside a very good range of other people's cheeses, they also sell a couple of their own made by Karen Hindle.

DECEMBER

Christmas dinner

Terrine of Beenleigh Blue with young mixed leaves and
roast sweet potatoes

Three mushroom tartlet with roast garlic and pine nut base, with a
cepe sauce, celeriac and potato mash, roast parsnips, Savoy cabbage
and chilli glazed carrots

Pears in a mulled wine syrup

Nibbles for a better class of finger buffet

Rosemary roast potatoes with spicy tahini sauce

Mini pizzas with red onions and Stilton (or olives)

Spinach and goat's cheese filo triangles

Mushroom and Brie tartlets

Roast tofu and pepper kebabs

Blinis with baked beetroot and baba ganoush

Blini rolls with cheddar and sun-dried tomatoes

Lemon curd tartlets

Chocolate grapes

A great supper when you've had too much fancy food

Winter pasta with Caerphilly and Cheddar.

Seasonal pleasure

Refusing to think about Christmas until 24th December

Christmas dinner

This is the menu which we have served for Christmas dinner at The Place Below for several years.

Christmas is a time when every action is over-full of symbolic significance. The number of Christmas cards you receive says how popular you are; the decorations on your tree say how stylish you are; where you choose to spend which bits of Christmas Day says who you love most. And of course what you eat, and what you give others to eat, says everything about what kind of human being you are.

Well, I think this is all a lot of nonsense, but a lot of people do get very worked up about what they are going to eat, and what they are going to serve others, on Christmas Day. What follows is a meal for everyone to salivate over and enjoy. What I deliberately do not try to do is to mimic the place of a turkey at the dinner table. The problem with large constructions of the nut loaf variety is that they tend to be too stodgy. However, it is important to have a good gravy for mopping up with the mash. I would not suggest that anyone tries to put this meal on the table at the same time as smoked salmon followed by turkey with all the trimmings; you will simply die of stress and exhaustion.

TERRINE OF BEENLEIGH BLUE
WITH YOUNG MIXED LEAVES
AND ROAST SWEET POTATOES

Beenleigh Blue is an English sheep's milk blue cheese made in Devon, amazingly delicious and widely available in good cheese shops which stock proper English cheeses. If you can't find it locally you can buy it by mail order from Neal's Yard Dairy in London. You can also use Roquefort, which produces an even richer result. In either case serve with a sweet white wine such as Sauternes – Chateau d'Yquem if you happen to have any lying around.

This is a recipe which also appears in *Food from The Place Below*, but it is such a brilliant part of a Christmas dinner that I had to repeat it.

You should start making this two days before you want to eat it.

SERVES 8

100 g (3½ oz) Lexia raisins
50 ml (2 fl oz) brandy
450 g (1 lb) Beenleigh Blue
350 g (12 oz) cream cheese
100 g (3½ oz) walnut pieces, lightly toasted

For the salad:

1 kg (2 lb) orange fleshed sweet potato, cut into fat chips
3 tbsp sunflower oil
Salt and freshly ground black pepper
400 g (14 oz) mixed leaves, e.g. rocket, mizzuna and curly endive
(the pale part only)
2 tbsp walnut oil

1. Soak the raisins in the brandy overnight.

2. The next day, crumble the blue cheese into a big bowl. Using your hands, mix in the other ingredients gently.

3. Line a 900 g (2 lb) loaf tin with clingfilm. Press the cheese mixture down into the lined tin. Wrap the surplus clingfilm over the top and weigh down well for several hours or overnight.

4. Preheat the oven to 220°C (425°F/Gas Mark 7).

5. Turn the terrine out and slice – I find this easiest with a serrated knife, using a sawing motion.

6. Toss the sweet potatoes in the sunflower oil and some salt and pepper, and lay out on a single layer on a baking sheet. Put in the preheated oven and roast until very soft and colouring at the edges. Ideally the sweet potatoes would still be a little warm when you serve the salad, but they are also fine at room temperature.

7. Toss the leaves in a little seasoned walnut oil and put a pile on each plate. Arrange a few bits of roast sweet potato randomly on top of them and top with a slice of the terrine. Garnish with a wedge of lemon.

THREE MUSHROOM TARTLET WITH ROAST GARLIC AND PINE NUT BASE, WITH A CEPE SAUCE, CELERIAC AND POTATO MASH, ROAST PARSNIPS, SAVOY CABBAGE AND CHILLI GLAZED CARROTS

If you are serving all the component parts of this meal, you can make the sauce, the tartlet cases and the pine nut purée for the tartlets the day before. The mushrooms can be fried a couple of hours before the meal, and the mash and the glazed carrots can be made a bit ahead of time. The roast parsnips and the very briefly cooked cabbage will both suffer from hanging around.

Three mushroom tartlet

This is a simple and quite flexible idea. The bases of individual tartlets are filled with a kind of savoury frangipane and topped with sautéed mushrooms. We do a similar tartlet with a base of ground almonds, basil and sun-dried tomato and topped with a mixture of different coloured cherry tomatoes and plum tomatoes. Neither the mushroom nor the tomato tartlet work well as large tarts for slicing – so stick to individual tartlets for these recipes.

You can use various wild mushrooms – pieds de mouton are especially good – if you can get hold of them. I have specified these three varieties both because they taste really good, and because they are now all cultivated and therefore relatively easy to get hold of.

The individual parts of the tarts (the pastry base, the pine nut mixture and the mushrooms themselves) can be prepared ahead of time, but the tartlets should not be put together until shortly before they are going to be re-heated or they will go a bit soggy.

SERVES 8

½ quantity (possibly more) of wholemeal pastry (see page xii) rolled out very thinly and baked blind in individual tartlet tins, approximately 10 cm (4 inches) diameter

1 bulb garlic
80 g (3 oz) pine nuts, lightly toasted
2 tbsp lemon juice
70 ml (3 fl oz) water
1 branch fresh thyme, stripped

Salt and pepper
Sunflower oil, for frying
350 g (12 oz) field mushrooms, cut into large chunks
350 g (12 oz) oyster mushrooms
350 g (12 oz) shitake mushrooms

1. Blind bake the individual tartlet cases (see page 248).

2. Pre-heat the oven to 200°C (400°F/Gas Mark 6).

3. Break the bulb of garlic into cloves but do not peel them. Spread out on to a baking sheet and put in the oven for about 15 minutes until they smell nutty and are a little soft when prodded. Allow them to cool and then peel them. (If you have overcooked them and they are very soft this can be quite a sticky business – but the taste will be good.)

4. Put the peeled, baked garlic in a blender with the toasted pine nuts, lemon juice, water, fresh thyme and a good pinch of salt. Whizz until smooth and then taste. You are looking for something quite assertive as it goes on in quite a thin layer. Adjust the seasoning with extra lemon juice or salt as necessary.

5. Next fry the mushrooms. They need to be fried in small batches on a high heat and you should season each batch as you go. If you try to fry too

many at once or over too low a heat they will sweat and go slimy, which is not the objective. The pan should remain fairly dry as you fry.

6. When all the mushrooms are fried you are ready to assemble the tarts. Divide the pine nut mixture between the blind-baked tartlet cases and spread it evenly over the base. Arrange the fried mushrooms on top, starting with the field mushrooms, then the oyster mushrooms and lastly the shitake mushrooms, which I think are most elegant if arranged bottom up.

7. Before serving, pre-heat the oven to 180°C (350°F/Gas Mark 4) and place the tartlets on a baking sheet in the oven for about 15 minutes. If you are serving them with roast parsnips or something else that needs a higher oven, then they can go in at the higher temperature for a shorter time, but keep a close eye on them as they will dry out quite quickly.

Cepe sauce

This is a really fantastic gravy – served with some cheesy bubble and squeak it makes a great supper, or it can also be a rich and elegant accompaniment to your Christmas dinner.

This sauce can happily be made a day or two in advance.

SERVES 8

50 g (2 oz) dried cepes
400 ml (14 fl oz) hot water, for soaking the cepes

1 tbsp sunflower oil
2 cloves garlic, crushed
½ small chilli, finely chopped, without the seeds
1 small onion, finely diced
200 g (7 oz) field mushrooms, finely diced
250 ml (9 fl oz) red wine
2 tbsp dark soy sauce

1 dsp arrowroot
Cold water to mix

1. Soak the cepes in the hot water for about 30 minutes.

2. In a saucepan, sweat the garlic, chilli and onion in the sunflower oil until soft. Add the diced field mushrooms and keep cooking until the mushrooms are soft and have given off their juice.

3. Add the wine and soy sauce. With a slotted spoon, take the cepes from their liquid and add them. Strain the liquid from the cepes through a fine sieve and add that also. Bring everything to the boil and simmer for at least 10 minutes with the lid off, allowing the sauce to reduce a little.

4. Mix the arrowroot with a few drops of cold water and add half of it to the sauce. Bring back to the boil, stirring well. If you would like the sauce to

be thicker, repeat the process with the rest of the arrowroot mixture, otherwise leave it as it is. Check the seasoning.

Celeriac and potato mash

This does not need to be made at the last minute, and will keep warm quite happily for an hour or so in a warming shelf.

SERVES 8

600 g (1 lb 5 oz) celeriac, peeled and diced
600 g (1 lb 5 oz) potatoes, peeled and diced
150 ml (5 fl oz) milk
100 g (4 oz) butter
Salt and freshly ground pepper

1. Boil the celeriac and potatoes in separate pans until each is tender, then drain.

2. Put the cooked celeriac into a food processor with the warmed milk and butter and whizz until smooth.

3. Mash the potato with a potato masher, then mix in the celeriac purée. (Don't whizz the potato in the blender, as it will go glutinous.) Season to taste with salt and pepper.

Roast parsnips

An essential feature of any serious winter celebration. People who think that they don't like parsnips have never had really well roasted parsnips. Sweet, crisp and chewy – a great contrast with the celeriac and potato mash and another excellent mopper-up of cepe gravy.

1 kg (2 lb) parsnips, peeled and cut lengthways. Smallish parsnips should
be cut once lengthways, larger ones may need to be de-cored if they look woody
in the middle, and then cut into four lengthways.
3 tbsp sunflower oil
Salt and pepper

1. Pre-heat the oven to 220°C (425°F/Gas Mark 7).

2. Bring a large pan of water to the boil. Boil the parsnips for about 10 minutes until almost tender. Drain thoroughly and toss gently (they may be quite breakable at this point) in the sunflower oil, salt and pepper. Spread them out on a large baking tray, making sure that they don't overlap each other. Put in the oven and check after about 20 minutes. If the undersides are beginning to colour, turn them over and leave for another 10 minutes. They should be going golden on both sides, and possibly a rather darker colour at the thin tips. They are then ready to serve.

(If you have boiled the parsnips for a little too long they will tend to fall apart when you turn them in the oil. They will also have absorbed additional water so they will take longer to roast. They will end up tasting excellent even if they don't look perfect, so don't despair.)

Savoy cabbage and chilli glazed carrots

Tossing the glazed carrots with the cabbage makes the sweet chilli flavour milder. For stronger contrasts keep the two vegetables separate. (There is also the question of how many vegetable dishes you can fit on the table.) I've also served the carrots with blanched cauliflower and broccoli and then tossed the whole lot in a mustard vinaigrette, and that is another excellent combination.

SERVES 8

500 g (1 lb) carrots, peeled and cut diagonally
25 g (1 oz) butter
1 clove garlic, crushed
½ a small chilli, de-seeded and finely chopped or ¼ tsp of chilli flakes
100 ml (4 fl oz) freshly squeezed orange juice
2 tsp caster sugar
Salt

1 medium Savoy cabbage, cored and finely shredded
2 tbsp olive oil
Salt and pepper

1. Put everything in the carrot section of the ingredients (carrots, butter, garlic, chilli, orange juice, sugar and salt) in a heavy-bottomed saucepan which has a close fitting lid.

2. Bring to the boil and simmer with the lid on for about 5 minutes until the carrots are nearly (but not quite) tender. Take the lid off, turn the heat up and cook fiercely, stirring constantly and keeping a watchful eye until the liquid has reduced to a sticky goo. Turn the heat off.

3. Meanwhile, bring a large pan of water to the boil. When it is boiling add the cabbage and bring back to the boil on as high a heat as possible. Boil for only about 1 minute, drain and toss in the olive oil and season.

4. Before serving, stir the glazed carrots into the cabbage and put in a warmed serving dish. (The easiest thing is to cook the carrots in something like Le Creuset and to use that as the serving dish.)

PEARS IN A MULLED WINE SYRUP

Pears in red wine can be either very ordinary or a really intensely flavoured hit of fruit flavours which is quite special. To make it delicious you must skimp neither on the quantity of wine, nor on the cooking time.

Really ripe pears are not so good for this recipe; if that is all you have you will need to reduce the cooking time of the pears very considerably.

Plums are delicious cooked in a similar way. You should cut a circle around their middle just skin deep; they should then be poached in the liquor in batches until they are tender (a much shorter time than for the pears) and then the syrup should be reduced in the same way.

This dish should be made the day before you want it and can happily be made a couple of days earlier if that's more convenient.

SERVES 8

8 firm pears
500 ml (18 fl oz) red wine
500 ml (18 fl oz) apple juice
1 stick cinnamon
3 cloves

175 g (6 oz) caster sugar

1. Peel the pears, leaving the stalk on, and put in a lidded saucepan (not aluminium) with the red wine, apple juice, cinnamon and cloves. The pears should be covered (or almost completely covered) by the wine and juice; if they are not, add a little water. Bring to the boil and simmer gently with the lid on for about 30 minutes.

2. Add the sugar and dissolve it. Bring back to the boil and simmer gently for a further 15 minutes. The pears should by this time be tender but not mushy. Take them out with a slotted spoon and put in a shallow dish.

3. Put the syrup back on a high heat and boil fiercely for about 30–45 minutes until the liquid has reduced to one third of its original volume. Pour it over the pears and leave overnight. Turn the pears over at least once so all parts of them get a good soaking in the reduced syrup. Serve cold with crème fraîche or clotted cream.

Nibbles for a better class of finger buffet

Obviously the easiest thing to do is simply to open a few packets of crisps and then let everyone get very drunk.

If, however, you are catering for a party where you want people to taste and enjoy what they are eating, then you are committing yourself to some serious time in the kitchen. It is always much more laboursome to produce good food in bite-sized pieces.

Nearly all of the recipes which follow are open to numerous variations. One thing to bear in mind is that it should be possible to eat finger food in your fingers – even if people still request plates to make private food stockpiles. Also, as people are eating one bite at a time, you are looking for quite strong flavours – so, for instance, beetroot and baba ganoush on blinis is better than the more obvious, but less intense, beetroot with sour cream and dill. The sweet tartlets are better with a lemon curd filling than with frangipane. A delicate base and a tasty top is the general theme.

All of the food which needs to be cooked at the last minute needs a hot oven, although slightly different temperatures are specified in different recipes. If you're doing more than one of the hot nibbles, they'll be fine if you cook them together at the same temperature. I think that a good proportion of a winter finger buffet should consist of hot food. This is less convenient for the person preparing the buffet, but much nicer for the people eating it.

All these recipes serve 20. If you do all of them you will have fed your guests with the equivalent of a full meal.

ROSEMARY ROAST POTATOES WITH SPICY TAHINI SAUCE

If you are only going to do one nibbly thing, then this should be the one. It is an extremely delicious combination and easy both to produce in large volume and to serve warm. You can find the sauce in *Food from The Place Below*, but I repeat the recipe here for convenience. The sauce can be made a day or two in advance.

Potatoes cooked in this way are our standard daily potato at Café @ All Saints – they are very easy to do, and a great accompaniment to quiches and pies – in fact we have a few customers who come in and simply eat rosemary roast potatoes for lunch. Is this the way forward for the 21st century chip butty?

The sauce

1 tsp chilli powder
2 cm (1 inch) slice fresh ginger root, peeled and grated
3 good cloves garlic, peeled and crushed
175 ml (6 fl oz) water
175 g (6 oz) honey
120 ml (4 fl oz) dark soy sauce
1 jar pale tahini
85 ml (3 fl oz) rice wine vinegar – this is very mild and is not the same thing
as rice vinegar; if you use another kind of vinegar, reduce the quantity

Put all the ingredients in a blender and whizz until smooth. It may seem rather liquid at first, but it thickens up over time.

The potatoes

Don't use proper new potatoes for this, but small main crop potatoes the same size as new potatoes, sold in the catering trade as 'mids'.

4 lb small potatoes, 'mids'
4 tbsp olive oil
1 tbsp dried rosemary
Salt and pepper

1. Pre-heat the oven to 220°C (425°F/Gas Mark 7).

2. Mix all the ingredients together and spread them out on a large baking tray, making sure they are only one deep. Use a baking tray with sides, or the oil will drip off and burn on the bottom of the oven. Roast in the oven for about 30 minutes until the potatoes are becoming crisp on the outside but tender in the middle.

Let them cool a little before passing them round on plates with little bowls of the spicy tahini sauce in the middle.

MINI PIZZAS WITH RED ONIONS AND STILTON (OR OLIVES)

You can make a big pizza and chop it up into little pieces, but this ends up very messy, and with a finger buffet you are looking for a measure of elegance.

The pizza dough

Make up a batch of dough according to the Pizza Dough recipe on page 111. Take it as far as the first rising (i.e. before you shape the dough). This will be more than you need for 20 tiny pizzas, so put any leftover dough in the fridge and make a pizza for two the next day.

Topping

2 tbsp olive oil
250 g red onions, halved and thinly sliced
1 clove garlic, crushed
1 tsp balsamic vinegar
1 sprig thyme, the leaves stripped from the stalk

Either 75 g ripe Stilton or 50 g pitted black olives, roughly chopped

1. Sweat the onions and garlic in the olive oil for about 15 minutes or more until the onions are very soft. Stir in the balsamic vinegar and thyme leaves and keep on the heat for a minute until the liquid from the vinegar has evaporated.

2. Pre-heat the oven to 230°C (450°F/Gas Mark 8).

3. Measure 20 15 g (½ oz) balls of dough. (If you don't have scales this accurate, or you can't be bothered to be so precise, the dough balls should be about the size of a fairly large grape). Working with a little flour sprinkled on your fingers, hold a ball in your hand and flatten it with your fingers so you have quite a thin flat disc and put this on an oiled baking sheet. Repeat with the other balls of dough. Divide the onion mixture between the pizzas and leave them to prove for at least 20 minutes in a warm place until they look a bit puffy.

4. Put them in the oven for 7 minutes. Take them out and put a tiny bit of Stilton on top of each one. Put them back in the oven for 1–2 minutes – not longer. Serve at once to guests with asbestos mouths. Otherwise, let them cool for a couple of minutes before passing them round.

Home made Pesto (*see page* xiii) and little pieces of de-seeded plum tomato make another excellent topping. We also often serve pesto and plum tomato on top of little croutons. To make the croutons, cut the crusts off a loaf and slice it thinly. Cut each of the slices in four and gently toss in some olive oil and salt and pepper. Spread out on baking trays, making sure the pieces do not overlap, and bake in a medium oven for about 15 minutes, turning them over after 10 minutes, until golden and crisp on both sides. Allow to cool and then put the topping on.

SPINACH AND GOAT'S CHEESE
FILO TRIANGLES

These simple pastries are quite similar to snacks you buy on the streets of Athens, except that there they would be made with feta rather than goat's cheese. If you do make it with feta, try to get hold of a feta made with sheep's milk – that seems to be more a guarantee of quality than whether or not the cheese is made in Greece.

Leek and Gruyère make another lovely filling for these parcels.

1 tbsp olive oil
250 g (9 oz) leaf spinach (frozen is fine), roughly chopped
1 clove garlic, crushed
80 g (3 oz) fresh goat's cheese e.g. Neal's Yard Perroche log, or good feta
A little freshly grated nutmeg
Salt and pepper

4 sheets filo pastry, about 25 cm (10 inches) by 18 cm (7 inches)
50 g (2 oz) butter, melted

1. Put the olive oil, spinach and garlic in a pan and cook, uncovered, over a medium/high heat until the spinach is cooked and most of the moisture driven off. (If you are doing this in larger quantities, you may have to drain some liquid off the spinach at the end.)

2. Take the spinach off the heat and mix with the goat's cheese and nutmeg. Season generously with salt and freshly ground pepper and taste.

3. Pre-heat the oven to 220°C (425°F/Gas Mark 7). Put a sheet of filo pastry on a work surface with the long side closest to you and brush all over with butter. Cut it into six strips parallel with the short side. Put a well-filled teaspoon of spinach mixture on each strip at the end closest to you. Fold the bottom right hand corner of the strip diagonally left and up, leaving a point on the bottom left of the strip. Then fold this point straight up

the left hand side, leaving a point this time on the right of the strip. Fold this straight up leaving the point on the left; and so on until you get to the end of the strip, leaving you (after a bit of practice) with a neatly formed triangle. Brush the outside with butter and put on a baking sheet. Repeat with the rest of the sheet of filo and the remaining three sheets, making 24 triangles in total.

4. Bake for about 15 minutes until the pastry is golden. Allow to cool for a few minutes before serving.

Professional party caterers often cook little pastries like these the day before, or even cook them in advance and then freeze them. Whilst this may be convenient, it does nothing for this kind of filled pastry, which should be eaten soon after being cooked.

MUSHROOM AND BRIE TARTLETS

By contrast with the filo triangles, the pastry for these tartlets, and the Lemon Curd Tartlets given on page 251 can happily be rolled out and blind-baked the day before.

Make a full quantity of the Wholemeal Pastry recipe on page xii. You will only need one third of it for 20 tartlets, so freeze the other two thirds separately for future use.

It really makes a big difference to use a decent unpasteurized ripe Brie. Much as I would like to be a fan of Somerset Brie, it just doesn't have the farmyard smell that you want from this kind of cheese. You may not use all the cheese I've specified in this recipe, but it's great stuff to have in the house.

Makes 20 tartlets

500 g (1 lb 2 0z) field mushrooms, fatly sliced
Sunflower oil for frying
Salt and pepper
250 g (9 oz) farmhouse Brie

1. Pre-heat the oven to 220°C (425°F/Gas Mark 7).

2. Roll out the pastry very thinly and drape over 10 tartlet moulds. I like the boat-shaped ones which are about 10 cm (4 inches) by 4 cm (1 inch) at their widest point. Press the pastry very firmly into the base and sides of each tin and then use the top of the tins to break it off cleanly. You then need another 10 moulds to press on top of the raw pastry so that it does not slip or bubble up when you cook it. Put into the oven for about 10 minutes until just cooked − the tartlets will go back into the oven briefly when they are filled so the pastry shouldn't be overcooked at this stage. Repeat for the next 10 tartlets. Note that you can only cook half as many in each batch as you have tartlet cases, so if you are cooking for a big party you need to get hold of a lot of tartlet cases.

3. Fry the mushroom chunks in the sunflower oil in small batches on a high heat so that they fry in the oil rather than steaming in their own juices. Season them well.

4. Put little bits of Brie in the bottom of the tartlets. Then put a fat chunk of fried mushroom on – two if they will fit – and then another bit of Brie. Put back in the oven for 5 minutes to heat, and then serve warm.

ROAST TOFU AND PEPPER KEBABS

This uses standard Place Below marinated and roast tofu, which I continue to think is not only really tasty, but is the only way of making this kind of tofu taste really good.

250 g (9 oz) block firm tofu, cut into 24 cubes
50 ml (2 fl oz) soy sauce
50 ml (2 fl oz) red wine
50 ml (2 fl oz) water
1 clove garlic, crushed
Small chunk of root ginger, peeled and diced finely

2 tbsp sesame oil
1 tsp Tabasco (more if you like it really spicy)

1 red pepper, cut into 8 strips and then each strip cut into 3
1 yellow pepper, cut into 8 strips and then each strip cut into 3
1 tbsp olive oil
Salt and pepper

1. Put the cut tofu in a bowl with the soy sauce, red wine, water, garlic and ginger and leave for at least 2 hours.

2. Pre-heat the oven to 220°C (425°F/Gas Mark 7).

3. When the tofu has marinated for long enough, take it out of the marinade (which you can use again, or use as seasoning in soups or sauces). Turn the tofu in the sesame oil and Tabasco and spread out on a baking sheet. Put in the oven for about 40 minutes until crisp. If there is a lot else in the oven it may take longer.

4. Turn the peppers in the olive oil and seasoning. Put in the oven for about 25 minutes until soft and colouring at the edges.

5. Make little kebabs on cocktail sticks, with a bit of pepper either side of the square of roast tofu. Serve warm or at room temperature.

BLINIS WITH BAKED BEETROOT AND BABA GANOUSH

These are simply mini versions of Blinis described on page 49, but without the mozzarella, and served at room temperature.

Make the blinis using a generous tablespoon of mixture for each one – you can fit several at a time in a frying pan. When they are cooked arrange them on a serving plate and top each one with a little baba ganoush and a small slice of baked beetroot.

BLINI ROLLS WITH CHEDDAR
AND SUN-DRIED TOMATOES

Make 6 larger blinis using a 50 ml (2 fl oz) ladle to measure out the batter for each one (you should have enough batter left if you have made a full quantity for the previous recipe). Take 3 or 4 dried tomatoes preserved in olive oil and chop them up very finely. Sprinkle them over the blinis and sprinkle some grated Cheddar over them. Roll them up like mini roulades and bake in a hot oven for about 5 minutes just so that the cheese melts. Cut them each into four diagonally and serve warm.

LEMON CURD TARTLETS

Make 20 sweet tartlet shells following the instructions for the mushroom tartlets, but using the Sweet Pastry recipe on page x.

The lemon curd also makes a delicious larger lemon tart. If you are making a large lemon curd tart it helps to return it to a 180°C (350°F/Gas Mark 4) oven for 10 minutes – this makes the curd set a little more and the tart easier to slice. There is no need to do this when making tartlets for a finger buffet since you don't have to slice them.

2 lemons, juice and zest
125 g (4 oz) caster sugar
50 g (2 oz) butter
3 eggs, lightly mixed together

In a small pan, heat the juice and zest of lemon, the sugar and the butter, until the butter has melted. Add the mixed eggs and stir continuously over a medium heat until the mixture begins to thicken. Take it off the heat and whizz with a hand-held blender (or in a food processor) to ensure the mixture is really smooth. Allow to cool and then spoon into the tartlet shells.

CHOCOLATE GRAPES

Seedless grapes are not remotely seasonal at this time of year, but they are extremely good covered in chocolate, so I swallow my principles and the chocolate grapes at the same time.

450 g (1 lb) seedless white grapes
110 g (4 oz) dark chocolate
Icing sugar

Cover a serving dish or tray with a bed of icing sugar. Melt the chocolate either in the microwave or in a glass dish suspended over some simmering water. Put a few grapes into the melted chocolate, take them out with a spoon and place them onto the icing sugar bed. When you have done this with all the grapes, put the tray in the fridge to chill thoroughly, then serve.

A great supper when you've had too much fancy food

WINTER PASTA WITH CAERPHILLY AND CHEDDAR

This recipe comes from a dish described to me by Sue Williams, partner of Vivian of Vivian's cheese shop in Richmond, London. Although Sicilian in origin, it works superbly with British cheeses such as a mild and crumbly Caerphilly and a melting Cheddar.

SERVES 4

2 tbsp olive oil
450 g (1 lb) onions, sliced
Large handful fresh sage leaves
Seasoning
275 g (10 oz) potatoes, cut into small (1 cm) cubes
225 g (8 oz) tagliatelle
225 g (8 oz) Savoy cabbage, finely sliced
450 g (1 lb) spinach, roughly chopped
225 g (8 oz) Caerphilly
100 g (4 oz) vegetarian Cheddar or Devon Oke, grated

1. Heat the oil in a large frying pan and cook the onions for 5 minutes until softened. Remove from the heat, stir in the sage and seasoning. Set aside and keep warm.

2. Bring a large pan of water to the boil and cook the potatoes for 2 minutes. Add pasta and cook for a further 8 minutes, until the pasta is almost cooked, then add the cabbage and spinach and cook for a further 2 minutes. Drain.

3. Place half the pasta mix in a serving dish, top with half the onion mix and half the cheese. Repeat the layers and serve immediately.

Seasonal pleasure: refusing to think about Christmas until 24th December

For my Christmas menu you may have to start thinking about Christmas before 24th December, but not very much before.

So why not enjoy October, November and especially December without thinking too much ahead of time about Christmas. Then, come Christmas itself, have a great time in the kitchen and even better time eating what you've made.

Then, turn back to the beginning of this book and next year cook some of the things you didn't get round to this year.

Happy eating!

Index

All Saints' dinner 205, 206–12
almond biscuits 76
apples 224
   and blackberry crumble 181
   fresh juice 12
   and raspberry cake 183–4
apricot, honey and Amaretto iced
   yoghurt 147–8
April 67–83
artichokes:
   globe, hollandaise 106–7
   Jerusalem, roast 27–30
asparagus:
   English dinner 84, 88–95
   English supper 85, 96–101
   gurgle of spring vegetables
      90–92
   and Jersey Royals tossed in
      tarragon butter 88–9
   in nori with dill dressing 113–14
   and tarragon and parsley risotto
      96–7
aubergines:
   charred:
      and buffalo mozzarella blini
         49–51
      purée, baba ganoush 127
   salad of roast Mediterranean
      vegetables with pasta 130–32
   with truffle oil, parmesan and
      rocket 169
August 153–65
August bank holiday dinner 153,
   154–9

autumn dinner 189, 190–97
autumn pudding with plums and
   fresh figs 196–7
autumn supper 189, 198–201
avocados:
   and Alfonso mangoes and baby
      gem lettuce salad, with a
      ginger and tahini dressing 98–9
   and baby gem lettuce, waxy
      potatoes and beef tomatoes
      salad with a saffron dressing
      195
   and cucumber and sorrel soup,
      chilled 154

baba ganoush 127, 250
banana and fig tarte tatin 211–12
banoffee pie 58–9
beans:
   broad:
      early summer vegetables with
         fresh herbs, olive oil, lemon
         and Caerphilly 120–21
         summer garden pasta 122
   green, in a tomato and honey
      vinaigrette 129
   haricot:
      and celeriac and roast garlic
         soup 25–6
      and garlic, truffled cappuccino
         190–92
Beenleigh Blue terrine, with young
      mixed leaves and roast sweet
      potatoes 230–31

beetroot:
  baked 219–21
  buttered, and blood oranges 52
  and potato and goat's cheese
    gratin 198–9
  and potatoes and fresh goat's
    cheese pizza 110–12
  and red onion ragout 219–20
biscuits:
  almond 76
  Cornish fairings 150–51
blackberries 182
  and apple crumble 181
blinis:
  with baked beetroot and baba
    ganoush 250
  charred aubergine and buffalo
    mozzarella 49–51
  rolls, with Cheddar and
    sun–dried tomatoes 251
brandy crème anglaise 41
bread:
  leek and Gruyère brioche 70–72
  olive oil 133–5
  pizza 110–12
  sourdough 11–13
Brie, warm:
  and plum sandwich 186–7
  on toast with plum compote
    185–6
brioche:
  leek and Gruyère, with tarragon
    and white wine sauce 70–72
  with strawberry jam 86–7
broccoli:
  gurgle of spring vegetables 90–91
  with olive oil and lime 199
  with pasta 81

purple sprouting, with lime hol-
    landaise 68–9
  salad 83
  summer garden pasta 122
bulghur with olive oil and lime 181
butternut squash:
  and chicory pancakes, with a
    Gruyère and white wine sauce
    34–6
  with ricotta and thyme pesto
    stuffing 192–3
  roast 27–30

cabbage 66, 83
  and pasta 81
  Savoy:
    with balsamic cream 210
    and chilli–glazed carrots 238–9
  with spaghetti with quick pesto,
    and roast potatoes 79–81
cakes:
  early strawberry and mascarpone
    100–102
  hazelnut meringue with raspberry
    sauce 175–6
  raspberry and apple 183–4
canapés, stuffed morels 103
carrots:
  and cauliflower, in tomato
    vinaigrette 73
  chilli glazed 238–9
  and coriander gateau with white
    wine and saffron sauce 141–2
  early summer vegetables with
    fresh herbs, olive oil, lemon
    and Caerphilly 120–21
  gurgle of spring vegetables
    90–92

mousse, with samphire and
young carrots vinaigrette
108–9
cashew and lentil pâté with
canteloupe melon, peaches,
avocado and a chilli and lime
vinaigrette 155–6
cauliflower:
and carrots, in tomato vinaigrette
73
and coriander soup, Luke's
Cornish 77–8
salad 83
celeriac:
and haricot bean and roast garlic
soup 25–6
and potato mash 236
cepes 189, 202–3
and field mushroom risotto 5–6
sauce (gravy) 235–6
Champagne cocktail 33
cheeses, British 224–5
cherry strudel 142–3
chickpeas, Ian's spiced 180
chicory:
and butternut squash pancakes,
with a Gruyère and white wine
sauce 34–6
and roast sweet potato and Cashel
Blue, warm salad 47–8
salad of bitter leaves and
oranges 7
chilli and lime vinaigrette 155–6
chocolate 23, 37–43
cake, Dorothy Goodbody's, with
chocolate sauce 37–8
grapes 252
and marmalade tart 42–3

and pear crème fraîche tart
200–201
and rosemary pot 39
sauce 38
with roast pears 200–201
terrine, iced, Jurgen Quick's
40–41
white, physalis 33
Christmas dinner 226, 229–40
Christmas supper 227, 253
Christopher Lloyd's rhubarb and
lemon tart 54–5
cider brandy and Dunkerton's
cocktail 86
cocktails:
Champagne 33
cider brandy and Dunkerton's 86
corn on the cob 177
Cornish fairings 150–52
courgettes:
gurgle of spring vegetables
90–92
pesto summer pudding 157–8
roast, pesto and mozzarella
sandwich with tomatoes and
watercress 137
salad of roast Mediterranean
vegetables with pasta 130–31
crème anglaise, brandy 41
crème brûlée, spiced gooseberry
116–18
Crottin de Chavignol with onion
marmalade 93–4
cucumber, sorrel and avocado soup,
chilled 154
custard, brandy crème anglaise 41

December 226–54

Dorothy Goodbody's chocolate cake
    with chocolate sauce 37–8
dried fruit compote with Greek
    yoghurt 18

early Spring supper 67, 77–82
early summer six course
    celebration dinner 105,
    106–18
Easter lunch 67, 68–7
eggs, scrambled:
    with morels and fried leftover
    new potatoes 86–7
    truffled, with roast parsnips 2–4
elderberry vinegar, spiced 163
English asparagus dinner 84, 88–95
English asparagus supper 85,
    96–101

February 22–43
fennel:
    and green pea soup with parsley
    and lemon 60–61
    gurgle of spring vegetables
    90–92
    and sweet potato and Caerphilly
    pie 56–7
figs:
    and banana tarte tatin 211–12
    fresh, and plums, autumn
    pudding 196–7
filo triangles, spinach and goat's
    cheese 246–7
finger buffet, nibbles 226, 241–52
Frances' salad of avocado, Alfonso
    mangoes and baby gem lettuce,
    with a ginger and tahini
    dressing 98–9

fruit:
    British 205, 224–5
    dried, compote with Greek
    yoghurt 18

garlic:
    baked 103
    and chilli roast potatoes 74
    gurgle of spring vegetables
    90–92
    and haricot beans, truffled
    cappuccino 190–92
    and pine nut base, for mushroom
    tartlet 232–34
    potatoes 27–9
    roast, and celeriac and haricot
    bean soup 25–6
ginger and tahini dressing 98–9
globe artichoke hollandaise 106–7
gooseberry crème brûlée, spiced
    116–18
grapefruit, pink, with Alfonso man-
    goes 86–7
grapes, chocolate 252
Gruyère and white wine sauce 34–6
gurgle of spring vegetables 90–92

harvest supper 1: 166, 169–76
harvest supper 2: 166, 177–81
hazelnut meringue cake with
    raspberry sauce 175–6
hollandaise, lime 68–9
hummus and roast pepper sandwich
    135–6

Ian's spiced chickpeas 180
ice cream:
    Sarah's spiced vanilla 148–9

strawberry 144–5
tayberry 146
iced yoghurt, apricot, honey and
Amaretto 147–8

January 1–21
Jerusalem artichokes, roast 27–30
July 124–51
June 105–23
Jurgen Quick's iced chocolate
terrine 40–41

kale, stir-fried, with cumin and
lemon 57
kebabs:
with morels and preserved
onions 102
roast tofu and pepper 249–50

Lebanese plate 126–9
leeks:
and Caerphilly potato cakes
216–18
and Gruyère brioche with
tarragon and white wine sauce
70–72
with pasta 81
and potato soup with Thai
flavours 63
lemon curd tartlets 251–2
lentils:
and cashew pâté with canteloupe
melon, peaches, avocado and a
chilli and lime vinaigrette 155–6
and pumpkin and sage soup
205–6
Puy, in a truffled balsamic
vinaigrette 130, 132

and sweet potato soup 63–4
sweet and spicy peasant soup
16–17
lettuce:
baby gem, salad:
and avocado and Alfonso
mangoes, with a ginger and
tahini dressing 98–9
and waxy potatoes, beef
tomatoes and avocado, with
a saffron dressing 195
and pea and mint soup 140
lime hollandaise 68–9
Luke's Cornish cauliflower and
coriander soup 77–8

mangoes, Alfonso:
and avocado and baby gem
lettuce salad, with a ginger and
tahini dressing 98–9
with lime juice 95
with pink grapefruit 86–7
March 44–65
marmalade 1, 19–21
and chocolate tart 42–3
onion 93–4
May 84–103
May Day breakfast 84, 86–7
meringue, hazelnut, with raspberry
sauce 175–6
morels 85, 102, 202
with pasta and baked garlic 103
with scrambled eggs and fried
leftover new potatoes 86–7
mozzarella, buffalo 49
mushrooms:
and Brie tartlets 248–9
field:

and cepe risotto 5–6
and coriander, clear soup
170–71
stuffed with roast tofu and
shallots 208–10
and roast tofu sandwich 138
and Stilton and pumpkin pie
221–3
three, tartlet, with roast garlic
and pine nut base 232–4
wild 189, 202–3
see also cepes; morels

nectarines, roast, with raspberry
sauce and crème fraîche
158–9
New Year feast 1–9
New Year's resolution supper 1,
10–18
nibbles, for finger buffet 226,
241–52
nori sausages with pepperonata and
arame 172–4
Not Valentine's night dinner 22,
25–32
November 205–25

October 189–204
olive oil bread 133–5
onion marmalade 93–5
oranges:
and bitter leaves, salad 7
and buttered beetroot 52
fresh juice 10
marmalade 1, 19–21
and rhubarb panettone pudding
31–2

pancakes, chicory and butternut
squash, with a Gruyère and
white wine sauce 34–6
panettone pudding, rhubarb and
blood orange 31–3
parsnips:
and Cheddar and rosemary soup
62
and potato mash 208
roast 27–30, 237
with truffled scrambled eggs
2–4
passion fruit syllabub 82
pasta:
with Caerphilly and Cheddar
253–4
with morels and baked garlic 103
quick sauces 81
pastry:
sweet x
wholemeal xii
pears 224
chocolate and crème fraîche tart
200–201
in a mulled wine syrup 239–40
roast:
with chocolate sauce 200–202
and Stilton sandwich 138–9
tarte tatin 8–9
peas:
early summer vegetables with
fresh herbs, olive oil, lemon
and Caerphilly 120–21
and fennel soup with parsley and
lemon 60–61
and lettuce and mint soup 140
and mint and mascarpone blob
92

sugar snap, gurgle of spring
vegetables 90–92
summer garden pasta 122
peppers:
pepperonata and arame 174
roast:
and hummus sandwich 135–6
with tabouleh 128
and roast tofu kebabs 249–50
salad of roast Mediterranean
vegetables with pasta 130–31
pesto xiii
and mozzarella sandwich with
tomatoes, watercress and roast
courgettes 137
quick, with spaghetti 79–80
summer pudding 157–8
physalis, white chocolate 33
pizzas:
mini, with red onions and Stilton
or olives 244–5
tiny, with beetroot, potatoes and
fresh goat's cheese 110–12
plums 185
compote, with warm Brie on
toast 186–7
and fresh figs, autumn pudding
196–7
jam 164–5
and warm Brie sandwich 186–7
potatoes:
asparagus and Jersey Royals
tossed in tarragon butter 88–9
and beetroot:
and fresh goat's cheese pizza
110–12
and goat's cheese gratin 198–9
cakes, leek and Caerphilly 216–18

and celeriac mash 236
fried, and scrambled eggs with
morels 86–7
garlic 27–9
and leek soup with Thai flavours
63
and parsnip mash 208
roast:
garlic and chilli 74
lime pickle 223
rosemary, with spicy tahini
sauce 242–3
with spaghetti with quick
pesto, and spring cabbage
79–80
salad 160–61
and baby gem lettuce, beef
tomatoes and avocado, with
a saffron dressing 195
summer garden pasta 122
see also sweet potatoes
pumpkin:
and mushroom and Stilton pie
221–3
and sage:
and lentil soup 206–7
risotto 213–15

raspberries 182
and apple cake 183–4
sauce 175–7
with roast nectarines 158–9
ratatouille with Asian flavours
178–9
rhubarb 53
and blood orange panettone
pudding 31–3
fool 75

and lemon tart, Christopher
  Lloyd's 54–5
risottos:
  asparagus, tarragon and parsley
    96–7
  field mushroom and cepe 5–6
  pumpkin and sage 213–15

saffron dressing 195
saintly sandwiches 124, 133–9
salads:
  baby gem lettuce, waxy potatoes,
    beef tomatoes and avocado
    with a saffron dressing 195
  bitter leaves and oranges 7
  broccoli 83
  cauliflower 83
  chicory, roast sweet potato and
    Cashel Blue 47–8
  Frances', avocado, Alfonso
    mangoes and baby gem lettuce,
    with a ginger and tahini
    dressing 98–9
  Lebanese plate 126–8
  mixed leaves with roast sweet
    potatoes 230–32
  potato 160–61
  roast Mediterranean vegetables
    with pasta 130–31
  summer 124, 126–32
  tomato 162
samphire and young carrots
  vinaigrette 108–9
sandwiches, saintly 124, 133–40
Sarah's spiced vanilla ice cream
  148–9
Savoy cabbage:
  with balsamic cream 210

and chilli glazed carrots 238–9
seasonal pleasures:
  autumn fruits 167, 182–4
  blackberries and autumn
    raspberries 167, 182–4
  British fruit with British cheeses
    205, 224–5
  cabbage family 67, 83
  chocolate 23, 37–44
  elderberries 153, 163
  grapes 167, 185
  ice cream 125, 144–51
  marmalade 1, 19–21
  morels 85, 102–3
  peas and broad beans 104,
    119–22
  plums 153, 164–5, 167, 185–7
  potatoes 153, 160–62
  refusing to think about Christmas
    until 24th December 227, 254
  soups 45, 60–65
  strawberries 105, 123
  tomatoes 153, 162
  wild mushrooms 189, 202–3
seaweed:
  asparagus in nori with dill
    dressing 113–14
  nori sausages with pepperonata
    and arame 172–4
September 166–87
shallots:
  roast 27–30
  and roast tofu stuffed field
    mushrooms 208–10
Shrove Tuesday dinner 44, 47–55
sorrel:
  and cucumber and avocado soup,
    chilled 154

gurgle of spring vegetables 90–92

soups:
celeriac, haricot bean and roast garlic 25–6
chilled cucumber, sorrel and avocado 154
clear field mushroom and coriander 170–71
fennel and green pea, with parsley and lemon 60–61
leek and potato, with Thai flavours 63
Luke's Cornish cauliflower and coriander 77–8
parsnip, Cheddar and rosemary 62
pea, lettuce and mint 140
pumpkin, sage and lentil 206–7
rich sweet potato and lentil 64–5
sweet and spicy peasant 16–17
truffled cappuccino of haricot beans and garlic 190–92

sourdough, daily 13–15
spaghetti with quick pesto, roast potatoes and spring cabbage 79–81

spinach:
buttered 141
and goat's cheese filo triangles 246–7
gurgle of spring vegetables 90–92

Spring supper 67, 77–82
squash see butternut squash
still winter supper 44, 56–9

strawberries:
in balsamic syrup 115

ice cream 144–5
jam 105, 123
and mascarpone cake 100–101

strudel, cherry 140–1
summer salads 124, 126–32
summer supper 124, 140–43
sweet pastry x

sweet potatoes:
and chicory and Cashel Blue warm salad 47–8
and fennel and Caerphilly pie 56–7
and lentil soup 64–5
roast:
salad 230–31
and tapenade and fresh goat's cheese sandwich 138

sweet and spicy peasant soup 16–17
syllabub, passion fruit 82

tabouleh, with roast peppers 128
tahini:
and ginger dressing 98–9
sauce, spicy 242–3
tapenade with roast sweet potato and fresh goat's cheese sandwich 138
tarragon and white wine sauce 70–72
tarte tatin:
fig and banana 211–12
pear 10–11
tayberry ice cream 146
terrine of Beenleigh Blue, with young mixed leaves and roast sweet potatoes 230–31
tofu, roast:
and mushroom sandwich 138

and pepper kebabs 249–51

and shallots, stuffed field
  mushrooms 208–10

Tokaji with cantuccini 33

tomatoes 162

  beef, baby gem lettuce, waxy
    potatoes and avocado salad
    with a saffron dressing 195

  dried 162

  and pasta 81

  pesto and mozzarella sandwich
    with watercress and roast
    courgettes 137

  pesto summer pudding 157–8

  and saffron and almond sauce
    27–8

  salad 162

  stuffed 162

  vinaigrette 73

truffle oil 2, 130, 169, 190–92

truffled cappuccino of haricot beans
  and garlic 190–92

truffled scrambled eggs, with roast
  parsnips 2–4

truffles 2–3

Uncle Tony's marmalade 1, 19–21

Valentine's night dinner 22, 33–6

vanilla ice cream, Sarah's spiced
  148–9

vegetables:

  early summer, with fresh herbs,
    olive oil, lemon and Caerphilly
    120–21

  roast winter 27–30

  spring, gurgle of 90–92

  summer garden pasta 122

  sweet and spicy peasant soup
    16–17

white chocolate physalis 33

white wine and tarragon sauce
  70–72

wholemeal pastry xii

winter pasta, with Caerphilly and
  Cheddar 253–4

winter supper dishes 44, 56–9,
  205, 212–23

yoghurt, iced, apricot, honey and
  Amaretto 147–8